REEDS FOR WIND

FROM THE MIND OF
TESHELLE COMBS

Copyright © 2025 by Combs Arts & Entertainment

All Rights reserved, including the rights of reproduction in print or online in any whole or partial form.

Manufactured in the United States of America.

Book layout and design by Combs Arts & Entertainment.

Hardcover ISBN: 979-8308921264

Paperback ISBN: 979-8308921127

To all my runners. Never run from yourself.

REEDS FOR WIND WORLD TERMINOLOGY

Crylia (*cr-ill-yuh*) – the realm of the superior griffin race

Cryl/Crylia (*cr-ill*) – a griffin (part eagle, part lion, part serpent) who can take on a humanlike appearance, some notably devoid of usual human emotions and affections

Tru (*troo*) – a network of human villages collected into one tribe

Tru-ori (*troo-oh-ree*) – Tru humans with golden features

Tru-hana (*troo-ha-nah*) – Tru humans with blue features

Gua (*gwah*) – goddess of water, patron goddess of the Tru tribe

Miror (*mee-roar*) – the world

Cza (*zah*) – the indisputable ruler of the Crylia, also known simply as the King

Black wings – the rarest of Cryl and the most severe and cunning

White wings – Cryl who are not as rare but very imperial and pretentious

Gold wings – elevated Cryl and often rare and noble

Silver wings – elevated Cryl who are often indifferent and intellectual

Gray wings – these Cryl are usually in the servant class and have more humanlike tendencies

Red wings – these Cryl are known for their impulsivity and cruelty

Krov vanya crystin - Pureblood Heir, literally translated 'Trail of Pure Blood' in Old Cryl

Zenith – the council that rules Miror

Bahari (*bah-ha-ree*)– one of the five branches of the Zenith

Ven – one of the five branches of the Zenith

SOME NAMES IN REEDS FOR WIND

Emyri Izela (*em-er-EE, iz-AY-luh*) – Tru-ori spy, Nkita's partner

Nkita Opas (*nick-EE-tuh, OH-pass*) - black wing, Grand Teth, First General, Em's partner

Rhaza (*rah-zah*) – leader of the Cryl rebels

Hrogar (*RO-gar*) – one-eyed gray wing rebel

Cyndr (*sin-der*) – Crylia slaver and rebel

Drosya (*JRO-syuh*) – an old crylia female Grounded

Dagon (*DAG-uhn*) – red wing rogue and friend of Nkita

Rizel (*rizz-zel*) – black wing monster

Miasi (*mee-YAH-see*) – Queen of the Tru

Tahlya (*TALL-ee-ah*) – white wing, offspring of Grigor

Grigor (*GREE-gor*) – silver wing, keeper of knowledge

Ikyi (*ee-KEE-yee*) – red wing, offspring of Grigor

1

The Day The Spy Was Not

Some see the world and think Gua is not in it. How can a little rain bring all this? But what would the reeds be without the river? What would the river be without the rain? Gua is good. And she brings life to all. Even those who do not know she is Gua.

He's looking for me.

I knew this, but I kept off the path, avoiding the patches of melting snow so they wouldn't show my footprints after I'd gone past them. The sun beat down with a strong fist. No more hiding behind clouds for now. Time to return the ground back to the warmth. But the cold season was still upon us. The sun would hide once more. It was only a matter of time.

"Iz?! Where are you?"

I ducked behind a berry bush, praying I wouldn't find any snakes there waking from their slumber. I plucked a few of the violet fruits and popped them between my teeth, sweet and bitter juice slipping down my throat as I hid.

"They're hardly ripe."

I jumped as Miasi whispered in my ear. She was crouching next to me, pulling the berries from the branches of our hiding place.

"What are you doing here?" I hissed. "Go away!"

She blinked those beautiful blue eyes at me. "I'm hiding."

"From what?!"

She shrugged. "Life."

I frowned. "You're going to get me in so much trouble."

"Would not be the first time, Izzy." Then she shushed me, peering over the bushes. "So enlighten me. Why are you hiding this time?"

I sighed. "Mahopi."

She grinned. "Your lover?"

"Stop that."

"Why are you hiding from him? I thought you liked Maho."

"I do. Really, I do."

"But...."

"He's too quick. For me." I shook my head. "It's hard to explain. You won't—"

"He wants to put you in his home and give you babies before the next year comes around. And you want to throw yourself off cliffs a few more times before that has to happen." She smirked. "Am I close?"

I groaned. "Yes."

"But when you do want babies, you want it to be with him?"

"Yes, I would like that. He's...."

"He's got those muscles...."

I chuckled. "Maybe you should marry him, eh?"

"Oh please. My father has planned for my mate since the day I was born."

"He'll be good. The King would not choose poorly for you, Miasi."

She frowned. "How can you be so sure, Iz?"

"He's the King. It's his job to bring wisdom to the people. And he will."

She was quiet, chewing her bitter berries. "The Cryl. Their advances are changing things for us."

I kissed her forehead, which I wouldn't be able to do if we weren't hiding in the bushes together. But hiding was just that. A chance to let pretenses down. A chance to act like no one was watching. "If he picks someone stupid, I'll object."

She grinned. "Oh, will you?"

"Yes. I will put my foot down."

"Oh dear. Frightful. He'd better watch out."

"I will bring a logical objection forth—"

Miasi pretended to shiver. "How could he resist? Such daring—"

"I'll begin with my deductions—"

"Such tenacity—"

"And end with a compelling conclusion!"

She giggled. "Which will be...?"

"Miasi should marry whomever she wants, and also maybe it should be Maho so I can thrash about the wildlands with no babies in my belly for all my days!"

We both screamed as the bushes were parted and Mahopi stood over us, glaring. "Emyri Izela! I thought you'd been taken!"

I rolled my eyes. "By who, Mahopi?"

"A winged Cryl!"

"Oh yes. Everyone, quickly. Be afraid. A black wing is coming."

"It's not funny, Izela. Cevae told me her uncle had his leg ripped clean off by a black wing."

I narrowed my eyes. "Where? While he was herding sheep?"

"In battle."

"Cevae is afraid of everything, Mahopi. Keep listening to her stories and you will be too."

"Too late for that," Miasi mumbled.

Mahopi scowled. "You dragged the Princess into this, too?"

Miasi shook her head. "I tried to tell her I had more important things to do—"

I gasped. "Oh my goodness! You did not!"

Mahopi crossed his arms. "Get out of there, both of you. Yahara is back from meeting with the King, and I *need* to know what assignment he's given her. What if it's exciting? Like...war general? Or head scout?"

I glared at him. "Yes. The *King of the Tru* is going to make *Yahara* take a position as a head scout."

"He might. You never know. And I can't very well leave you here to be eaten by black wings."

"Ready?" I whispered to Miasi while Maho blabbered on, grabbing her hand and slowly locking our fingers together.

"Oh, most certainly."

"Go!"

And we scrambled to our feet and darted further into the forest, past the little creek with the high reeds, past the knotted trees with the raised roots, past the icicles dripping off the branches of the silverbarks, until Mahopi's cries were nothing but wind at our backs.

2

THE DAY THE GENERAL CARRIED THE SPY

"Emyri Izela. If you don't show yourself this very instant, there will be a world of retribution to pay. Do not test me, woman." Nkita Opas stepped light-footed through the forest outside the Queen's Home, his tattered cloak flowing over the twigs and tree roots.

"A bit early for threats, is it not?"

I was indeed hidden from plain sight, taking advantage of the long shadows the taller trees cast in the morning light.

Nkita swiveled when he heard my voice and approached slowly, his lilac eyes pinning me down. "What do you think you're doing?"

I refused to flinch as I glared back at him. "Taking a walk."

"You're running from me, Em. Again."

"I didn't *run*," I argued. "It's just a walk."

He crossed thick arms. "Then why are you *standing still*, swathed in shadows?"

"You're dictating how I walk now?"

"Fine. I concede you're not running. Why are you hiding?"

Why am I hiding? Because it's what I do. And I need to stay practiced. I need to be sure that if something were to happen, something unexpected, I could slip into a forest and be gone. "It's just a habit. It has nothing to do with you or with us."

"Some habits need to die." He held out his hand. "Come here."

I studied that outstretched hand for a brief moment. I knew that even slight hesitation would wound him, prideful as he pretended to be. But I couldn't help who I was, no matter how much I wanted to be reckless and confident and unapologetically enamored. I was not that sort of lover. Too much had happened. Too much would happen still.

I took his hand, his fingers half covered in woolen gloves and the black metal of his armor over that. Perhaps Nkita didn't realize how strangely terrifying it was to the Tru to see a black wing in Cryl armor strolling about the forest. But I knew under that armor, beneath corded muscles and hollow bones, was a heart that meant no ill will to my people simply because they were mine.

"Is it the armor?" he asked.

I narrowed my eyes at him. "How did you know I was thinking about that, General?"

"I am beginning to know you more and more, Em."

"Because we're mates?"

"Because I am in love with you." We walked into the sunlight, the flickers shifting and turning as they mingled with the cool blue shadows. "You're always more skittish when I wear it."

"It's necessary. And you're often wearing it because you should."

"I can be outfitted in Tru armor if it brings you some peace."

I scoffed. "Our armor is nothing compared to yours. You're safer dressed as a Cryl unless we need to be in disguise. Not only is your metal sturdier, but you'll be less obvious if you need to blend in among other Cryl."

"A black wing is never less obvious, Em."

I examined the strong cut of his jaw and the tiny slivers of golden scars formed along his cheekbone and chin. "You will need to look like yourself...if the rebels are to make you their Cza."

"This again?"

"Yes, this again. It's important—"

"*You're* important."

"I'm not any Vessel, Nkita. Come on. I am hardly even Tru. Hardly a spy anymore. I could not even be punished correctly. Yet you and Queen Miasi truly insist I am some...some future Tonguekeeper?"

"You are. And that's just one of the many, many reasons you cannot keep disappearing on me. Even if it's for harmless morning walks."

I sighed. "If we can't agree on anything else, let's at least mobilize some sort of forces to find Drosya. I think we all agree it's our utmost priority to have her safe."

Nkita nodded. "Your Queen is setting up a scouting team."

"And you'll go with them?"

"I'm not leaving your side."

"You'd be best—"

"The Hresh came here looking for you, Em. They had you in their clutches. I'm not going anywhere."

"They were looking for *you*, Nkita. I am nothing but a Grounded to them."

"It's only a matter of time before the Cza figures out who you are. If we discerned it, he will too."

"And an army of rebels at your disposal? Would that not make me more safe against his advances? Imagining of course that I am this Vessel...."

Nkita stopped walking. "You are not listening, Emyri."

I faced him. "You are correct. I most certainly am not."

"I can't be the Cza if I'm going to protect you. I can't."

I stopped at that, my mind turning over his choice of words. "You...*can't*?"

"Precisely."

"Why not?"

"It's severely complicated."

I nodded. "You'd like to withhold the truth from me. That's what you mean by complicated."

"You're cross with me."

"Yes." I put my hand on his chest, the metal of his armor cold against my palm. He'd worn this very thing when he tore his talons into the bodies of my people once. And he'd worn it while he defended them as well. When the Cza took his wing. When I was used to torture him. *What will he face wearing it now?* "I withhold the truth as well. It's necessary. To keep your secrets as I keep mine."

He put his hands on my waist and pulled me closer. "How long will you be the spy and I the General, Emyri Izela? When will you truly decide to be my mate?"

"I've decided. You know this."

"I don't believe you." He tilted my chin up to him, his eyes flashing as he put his lip to mine, his tongue searching my mouth as if he could coax my secrets to fall free. "I shall have to investigate this claim more carefully."

I grinned. "An investigation? Sounds...foreboding—"

I squealed as he hoisted me into the air without warning, throwing me over his shoulder as he marched back toward our room in the Queen's Home.

Fine. I squirmed, trying to escape. But Nkita held me tighter and took a bite out of my rear as he carried me. *I suppose I'll stay for one more day. But just one.*

"You are. And that's just one of the many, many reasons you cannot keep disappearing on me. Even if it's for harmless morning walks."

I sighed. "If we can't agree on anything else, let's at least mobilize some sort of forces to find Drosya. I think we all agree it's our utmost priority to have her safe."

Nkita nodded. "Your Queen is setting up a scouting team."

"And you'll go with them?"

"I'm not leaving your side."

"You'd be best—"

"The Hresh came here looking for you, Em. They had you in their clutches. I'm not going anywhere."

"They were looking for *you*, Nkita. I am nothing but a Grounded to them."

"It's only a matter of time before the Cza figures out who you are. If we discerned it, he will too."

"And an army of rebels at your disposal? Would that not make me more safe against his advances? Imagining of course that I am this Vessel...."

Nkita stopped walking. "You are not listening, Emyri."

I faced him. "You are correct. I most certainly am not."

"I can't be the Cza if I'm going to protect you. I can't."

I stopped at that, my mind turning over his choice of words. "You...*can't*?"

"Precisely."

"Why not?"

"It's severely complicated."

I nodded. "You'd like to withhold the truth from me. That's what you mean by complicated."

"You're cross with me."

"Yes." I put my hand on his chest, the metal of his armor cold against my palm. He'd worn this very thing when he tore his talons into the bodies of my people once. And he'd worn it while he defended them as well. When the Cza took his wing. When I was used to torture him. *What will he face wearing it now?* "I withhold the truth as well. It's necessary. To keep your secrets as I keep mine."

He put his hands on my waist and pulled me closer. "How long will you be the spy and I the General, Emyri Izela? When will you truly decide to be my mate?"

"I've decided. You know this."

"I don't believe you." He tilted my chin up to him, his eyes flashing as he put his lip to mine, his tongue searching my mouth as if he could coax my secrets to fall free. "I shall have to investigate this claim more carefully."

I grinned. "An investigation? Sounds...foreboding—"

I squealed as he hoisted me into the air without warning, throwing me over his shoulder as he marched back toward our room in the Queen's Home.

Fine. I squirmed, trying to escape. But Nkita held me tighter and took a bite out of my rear as he carried me. *I suppose I'll stay for one more day. But just one.*

3

The Day The  Spy Spied

The strangest of things occurred when I was with First General Nkita Opas. When I was really with him. When my legs were tangled in his and my hands could trace the scars along his rippling back. When he had already pulled every bit of desire from my body and satisfied every need, soothed every pain. When I had kissed the slick skin along his neck and chest and my scalp was still throbbing from the tension of his fingertips in my hair.

When I was with him in those moments...I felt...nothing.

Not a dull blankness. No. I felt as if my body had expired, floating on a cloud of peace. As if my mind had emptied itself of every thought it ever held. There was no hum of bustling worries, no buzz of fears and flaws. All was still. I was still. I was nowhere.

Nkita took my hand and kissed my wrist. "Sleep," he urged me.

I let my eyes flutter closed. And I did sleep, even though it was the middle of the day. I slept until I felt Nkita stir, until I heard him dress. I peeked at him when he wasn't facing me just so I could see the scar he'd earned when the Cza took his wing. It ran deep and angry red down his shoulder blade. Whenever I saw it, I felt not rage, but unmatched fear. The Cza had used me to do it.

As soon as Nkita left the small room we shared, I leaped from the bed and dressed. Then, I tiptoed down the corridor after him. I kept in the shadows as he knocked on the door of Miasi's meeting room.

"Why are we sneaking?"

I gasped as Yahara whispered in my ear.

"Keep your voice down."

"I am literally whispering, Izela."

"Whisper softer. I don't want to be found out."

"You're spying? In the Home of the Queen?" She shoved my shoulder.

"Of course I'm spying in the Home of the Queen, Ya. How do you think I learn anything, hm?"

"That's how you got in trouble."

"That's how I get people I love out of trouble."

"Is that what you're doing right now? Who are you getting out of trouble?"

"I don't *know* until I spy. Now go away."

No one could hear what went on in the Queen's meeting room unless of course they had their own strategic hiding places. I crawled into the secret space I'd dug into the wall of my old room behind the bookshelf. Then up the makeshift ladder and to the gap between the ceiling and the wall. I perched there, my legs dangling. I used to listen to Miasi's father hold his meetings in that exact spot. Some things never changed.

"It smells weird in here," Yahara hissed, bumping me as she plopped beside me.

"You followed me?!"

"Shh. You'll give away our positions."

I glared at her as I quieted so I could hear the words being said. Nkita and Miasi were speaking with hushed voices, as if they worried they'd be overheard.

"The scouts will leave as soon as the snow falls."

"Why wait?" Nkita asked.

"The snow gives the Tru a bit more protection."

"Are you really basing your decisions as a leader on a fake goddess, Miasi?"

I could feel the tension in her voice. Gua was not fake, and I knew our Queen was not happy to hear her spoken of that way. "I am basing my decision on our ability to hide our movements in the snow, Nkita."

He sighed. "Very well."

"We have to make sure they are not picked off by Cryl. Something you have never had to consider when sending out scouts."

"I said 'very well'."

I had never heard Miasi so upset, so…harsh and commanding. "You will remain with Emyri Izela, of course."

"Of course. I cannot leave her side. Even this is too much distance."

"If the Cza gets his hands on her, it will be worse than if he finds the Tonguekeeper. She is the future."

"I understand. And I will protect her with my life."

A pause from Miasi. When she spoke again her words were careful. "Or…Nkita, you could…."

"It is not an option. It will never be an option. If you bring it up again, I will take Emyri and leave you and this place behind."

"I understand…."

"I don't think you do, young Queen. I will *never* do it. Never. And if you tell Em that it is an option, you have sealed your own fate."

"Are you threatening me, General?"

"For Em? Yes. I am."

"You could let her make her own choices."

"She will choose the selfless option. Em will always choose the selfless option. And I am unwilling to allow her to do so. The answer is no. The answer is never." He paused, and it made both Yahara and myself shiver when he spoke again. "If I must choose between you and Emyri Izela—if I must choose between any living being and Emyri Izela—you will be dead where you stand. I cannot make it more clear."

"Your Crylia ways make you bond to your mate," Miasi said, regaining her composure. "I understand."

"You are a good Queen, Miasi. Better than your father was King. But you understand nothing between her and me. It would do you well to remember that as you make your arrangements."

"And you would do well to remember who you are speaking to, General."

"A Royal is a Royal is a Royal. You are all the same."

"And you, Pureblood Heir, are no different than I. No matter how hard you pretend or how furiously you cling to the destiny of another."

"I will bring destiny to its knees for her. And you, Tru Queen, are no different."

Yahara and I sat in silence after the General left. Finally, my sister swallowed.

"I've never heard anyone talk to Miasi like that."

"Me neither."

"What...are they hiding from you, Iz? What can't you know?"

"I'm not yet sure, Ya."

"But you'll find out. Won't you?"

I steadied myself, my mind made up. "Oh, I will find every hidden answer. That's what I do best."

4

THE DAY THE GENERAL CARRIED THE SPY

I hurried out of my hiding place, just in time for Miasi and Nkita to exit the meeting room and just in time for Mahopi to round the corner, his blue hair in a fresh, tightly woven braid down his back, his handsome face drawn in concern.

"Queen Miasi. Excuse me."

"Mahopi." Miasi frowned. "What is wrong?"

"Something...."

"Show me," Yahara said, moving forward without waiting for anyone to command her to do so. "Queen Miasi, please wait here."

Our Queen nodded. "Be safe, please."

I hurried behind Yahara and Maho, and Nkita needed no invitation to follow as well.

"The waters have shifted," Mahopi explained.

"East to west?"

Mahopi shook his head. "West to east, east to west, and back around again. Over and over."

"Let's go up and see," she replied.

"What are they doing?" Nkita asked me.

"We Tru can tell the changes coming from the sky," I explained. "And how it plays upon the waters. We use it to make predictions."

"The sky speaks to you?"

I nodded. "Gua has her ways. You'll see. Then you'll understand."

We made it to the center of the Queen's Home and climbed the tall ladder to the keep that sat like a nest atop the structure.

Once we were all high enough, we looked out over our surroundings. "There," Mahopi said, pointing at the lakes surrounding us. "Something...strange."

"Look," I whispered to Nkita. "The ripples along the water's surface show how the wind is turning in the subtlest ways. Even before the clouds move. Even before its breeze strikes your face."

"I...see...."

"When Cryl are coming, we can tell the wind picks up in gusts from the power of their wings. The more Cryl, the easier to detect. They almost always fly in unison, their wings flapping at the same intervals when they scout. It gives us time to hide. But...the patterns are not supposed to shift so quickly."

"How do you know it's not an impending storm?" Nkita's careful lilac eyes scoured the water. "How do you know it's Cryl?"

"The storm blows steadier, with the rhythms of Miror. The Crylia move the water in short bursts from the pulsing of their wings in unison. But this...makes no sense."

Yahara frowned. "It looks like chaos. But, see how the ripples turn back on themselves? It's like Crylia are coming from every direction, flying at—"

"Multiple heights," Mahopi finished. "But they've never flown like—"

"We need to go," Nkita said, interrupting Maho.

My blood ran cold, my heart dropping into my stomach. "What are they doing, General?"

"If there are Cryl coming from many directions, flying at many heights, there has been a raze order."

Yahara stared at Nkita. "What do you mean? Raze order?"

"They will raze."

"Raze *what*?"

"Everything and everyone. Every home, every stone, every blade of grass."

"Nkita"—my voice trembled—"how do we stop it?"

"We don't."

"Then how do we survive it?" I refused to believe we would let the Home of the Queen be destroyed.

"We run."

"We cannot evacuate every blade of grass, Nkita—"

Mahopi shook his head. "West to east, east to west, and back around again. Over and over."

"Let's go up and see," she replied.

"What are they doing?" Nkita asked me.

"We Tru can tell the changes coming from the sky," I explained. "And how it plays upon the waters. We use it to make predictions."

"The sky speaks to you?"

I nodded. "Gua has her ways. You'll see. Then you'll understand."

We made it to the center of the Queen's Home and climbed the tall ladder to the keep that sat like a nest atop the structure.

Once we were all high enough, we looked out over our surroundings. "There," Mahopi said, pointing at the lakes surrounding us. "Something...strange."

"Look," I whispered to Nkita. "The ripples along the water's surface show how the wind is turning in the subtlest ways. Even before the clouds move. Even before its breeze strikes your face."

"I...see...."

"When Cryl are coming, we can tell the wind picks up in gusts from the power of their wings. The more Cryl, the easier to detect. They almost always fly in unison, their wings flapping at the same intervals when they scout. It gives us time to hide. But...the patterns are not supposed to shift so quickly."

"How do you know it's not an impending storm?" Nkita's careful lilac eyes scoured the water. "How do you know it's Cryl?"

"The storm blows steadier, with the rhythms of Miror. The Crylia move the water in short bursts from the pulsing of their wings in unison. But this...makes no sense."

Yahara frowned. "It looks like chaos. But, see how the ripples turn back on themselves? It's like Crylia are coming from every direction, flying at—"

"Multiple heights," Mahopi finished. "But they've never flown like—"

"We need to go," Nkita said, interrupting Maho.

My blood ran cold, my heart dropping into my stomach. "What are they doing, General?"

"If there are Cryl coming from many directions, flying at many heights, there has been a raze order."

Yahara stared at Nkita. "What do you mean? Raze order?"

"They will raze."

"Raze *what*?"

"Everything and everyone. Every home, every stone, every blade of grass."

"Nkita"—my voice trembled—"how do we stop it?"

"We don't."

"Then how do we survive it?" I refused to believe we would let the Home of the Queen be destroyed.

"We run."

"We cannot evacuate every blade of grass, Nkita—"

He put a strong hand on my arm. "I don't care about anything but you, Em."

I looked him in the eyes. "I am not leaving my family to *die*."

"Then choose who your family is right this moment. Because we are leaving."

"We cannot—"

"*Emyri*!" He roared so loudly that I stumbled backward. Striated lines of fur crept up his neck, his irises tightened to slivers, his very teeth pointed. "*Now*."

I inhaled a shaky breath. "Yahara, Miasi, Cevae, Mahopi, Beni." I could not believe it. That I was choosing, in one simple breath, who would live and thus who would be left behind to die.

Nkita pointed at Mahopi. "Collect Cevae and Beni. You have mere moments."

Mahopi left without a word, sliding down the ladder.

"I will...go home," Yahara said, her voice strained.

"Ya—"

"I won't leave my child and my partner," she said. She put a hand on the back of my head and pulled my forehead to hers. "Be safe; be smart. The water suits you, Izela."

I swallowed past the dread forming in my chest. "The... the rivers are yours, Yahara. Take care of them."

Then she released me and shoved Nkita's armored chest. "Don't let her die, monster. Do your job."

As soon as Yahara left down the ladder, Nkita took both my shoulders in his hands. "I need you to listen to me for once, woman. Listen all the way."

"You're scaring me, Nkita."

"It is the time to be afraid."

I shivered. "What...what is going to happen?"

"They will come. And they will annihilate everything in their search for me and for the Tonguekeeper. The Hresh travel in clusters of three, maybe four. But this is not the Hresh. This is what comes after. A battalion. I...cannot fight them all."

"You need an army."

"We need to evade them. It's the only way."

My eyes filled with tears. "They will kill Tru who have done *nothing*, Nkita. Families with children and elders, mothers with swollen bellies. We have to warn them."

"We cannot."

I shook my head and reached up so my hand rested on his sharp jaw. "Please. Hear my heart, Nkita. We have to try. *Please*."

He groaned, as if straining against some force I could not feel, like my heart had placed chains around his. What hurt me brought him pain. What tore at my soul ripped his to shreds.

With another groan, he pressed his mouth to mine. "You go with Miasi and Mahopi. Keep out of sight, as close to the ground as you can. And keep to the water's edge when possible."

"Nkita—"

"I'll warn who I can."

"How will I find you—?"

"If I live, I will find you."

"Don't *say that*."

"If I die, you must find the Tonguekeeper and remain with her until it's time." He took my face in his hands, his fingers reaching into my hair. "No matter what, do not let the Cza have you, Em. Fight that fate at any cost."

I could not keep the tears from slipping down my cheeks. "Come with me." My voice cracked. I wanted things that could not fit in the same reality. For my people to be safe....and for Nkita to be at my side. "Or let me come with you." But I knew what he would say. He was faster without me. Miasi needed me now more than ever. With Yahara gone....

"I will warn your people." He kissed me one last time. "For you."

Then, the black wing General leaped off the entire height of the Queen's Home, took a horse that wasn't his, and disappeared into the trees.

5

The Day The  Truth Burned

My limbs shuddered, my stomach tightening and my head reeling as I descended the ladder, and found Miasi stuffing things into an ordinary satchel. Something was…wrong. But there was no time for me to explore it, no time for me to communicate what my body was struggling to endure.

I rushed to her side. "Mia—"

"Ya told me," she said, her focus absolute. "Are you ready to leave?"

I nodded, trying my best to ignore the shallow strain of my breathing.

"I need one more thing," Miasi said. "We can get it on the way."

"Alright. Hurry."

I followed her as we raced through her Home. She must have told most of her helpers to flee because almost nobody remained. She stopped in one of the rooms that no one ever bothered to enter. It was filled with archaic books and maps and relics of times when Tru were not hunted, but thrived.

She threw one of the shelves over and watched as it fell to pieces, colliding with the floor. Then, she sorted through the shards of wood until she found a small metal box. After shoving it in the satchel, she nodded. "Let's go—"

I was already tugging her toward the doors, moving as fast as my legs could carry me. Beni, Cevae, and Mahopi were waiting outside, Maho pacing as if his nerves were on fire.

"Where's the Cryl?" he asked. "He said we had moments—"

"He will catch up with us," I said, embarrassed at how shaky my voice sounded to my own ears.

"What? He left?" Maho scoffed. "Probably to join the attack. He probably organized this whole—"

"Shut up, Maho," I said calmly. "There's no time to fight. There is only time for running."

"There are secret routes," Miasi said. "For royalty. Do you remember them, Izela?"

I nodded. "Of...of course." Miasi had broken sacred rules to show them to me when we were children. Not because I was supposed to be some important Tongue-keeper—we couldn't have known any of that back then—but because we were friends. She'd been lonely with her secrets, and I'd already begun collecting mine.

"We follow Iz," Miasi said, her calm voice the decision maker we all needed. She nodded at me.

I took off, headed to the east. If storms came, we'd be running into them headlong, but that was part of the reason the Tru elders hid the routes in that manner. They were treacherous. No one would expect us to run into storms.

"The Crags are this way," Cevae whispered to no one, running beside us. "We can't...we can't go through the Crags."

"Keep up," was all Beni said. He never spoke much, but he was the most constant friend. "Don't think. Just run."

Trust. They trusted I would lead them well, and I would. Except for what they did not know. Except for the truth I knew was waiting up ahead. Except for what I'd have to do once we reached the fork just outside the Crags. Miasi knew as well, yes, but she said nothing, her composure, as always, intact.

I kept my legs and arms pumping even as the wind changed around us. The Cryl army was closing in. The leaves of the trees were losing their grips on their branches. The animals ran opposite us, headed away from the wrath that would be raining down on the land. I wept for them. For us all. But I kept running forward.

Finally, up ahead loomed before us...the Crags of Woe, so named for the many, many Tru who'd lost their limbs or their lives trying to traverse them. The white stone of the jagged cliffs rose up out of the ground, fog thick and heavy covering the ravines below so that the perilous structures appeared to be rising out of nowhere.

"I don't think we should," Cevae said, holding my hand and squeezing. "Iz, let's go back."

I took a deep breath. "I...am sending you a different way, Vae." The truth hurt more than I thought it might. And it did not help that my heart was beating furiously out of rhythm, the sound of my own pulse thunderous in my ears.

She blinked at me. "What...what do you mean?"

"You, Mahopi, and Beni. You need to go down into this tunnel. Stay low and take the east first, then the west, and west again. You will come up safe in the village of Kiepo. But do not speak to anyone. Do not tell them about the tunnels. Instead get water and food and return. Travel north until you cannot anymore. Then, you will be safe—"

"We're not splitting up," Mahopi said, grabbing my arm so that he held me on one side as Cevae held the other. "We'll protect Miasi *together*."

"You have to listen—"

"Why would the Queen go with *you*, Izela?" As Mahopi spoke, his tone changed, his eyes narrowed, and his nostrils flared. And his truth spilled. "You betrayed our people. Took our king from us. You...you made an alliance with our enemy. I'm not letting her go with you. Not alone."

"Mahopi, quiet your heart," Miasi spoke up. "I have made my choice. With my guard, Pino gone, I must choose the person I most trust. And we must go a way no one knows. Emyri Izela is the only one who knows this way besides me. If I am hurt, she will make sure I make it to my destination safely. You cannot do that for me, Maho. And though you believe coming with me will help, it will only deter us. We need to travel relentlessly."

"But I—"

"You have just voiced your prejudice toward the one person who can help me now. I cannot believe you will protect her. You are holding hate. You cannot hold my trust." She squared her shoulders. "Rarely do I have to enforce my own commands. But you will take Cevae and Beni. And you *will* go. Until we meet again."

I watched as Mahopi's heart crumbled, as Cevae's fear clouded her tear-brimmed eyes, as Beni accepted his fate in silence.

"Be safe," I warned them.

Cevae kissed Miasi's hand and then threw her arms around my neck. "You are doing the right thing," she whispered into my ear. "See you soon."

I choked back tears as three of my dearest friends stumbled their way into the tunnels beneath the ground.

Miasi took my hand.

"I will get you across," I told her.

"No, Emyri Izela." She pulled me forward toward the Crags. "I will get *you* across."

6

The Day The  Helpless Fled

"If we had wings like the Crylia, this would be easy," Miasi said, slipping on her arse. She would have slid down the rest of the muddy slope if I hadn't grabbed her by the back of her dress and held. My other hand gripped a rock formation behind me, my palm scraping as I squeezed. My heart still pursued its pounding, and my body still flashed between icy cold and searing hot. But, I had work to do. I had to get my Queen safely through this harsh land.

"If we had wings like the Crylia," I grunted, pulling my Queen to her feet, "we'd be stuck underneath one of their males."

Once she found her footing, Miasi gripped my free hand and pulled me up beside her, chuckling. "You've already managed that, Iz."

"I don't feel very stuck, Mia. Believe me."

She brushed the mud from my face and frowned. "You do love him?"

"I...do. Very much."

"Has he earned it?"

"More than you could know...." I swiped at the perspiration beading on my forehead.

"Then...then we will have to marry you when this is all over." She nodded, her decision made. "A Tru wedding."

"Really, Miasi?"

"He may have earned your love, Izela. But you earned mine a long time ago." She put her hands on her hips, looking ahead to the long way we still had to travel. We were keeping low in the Crags, the fog giving us cover. But a wrong turn, and we'd be lost for months.

"I don't think I'll be a very good wife."

"You've always thought that."

"Well, I've been right so far. I'm a terrible mate. We've spent more time apart than together. Because of me."

"Just because you are complicated does not mean you aren't worth being pursued."

"I fear he'll be pursuing me all his days."

"Mm. Not to frighten you with my powers of Queenly perception, Izela but...you care to tell me what's wrong?"

"Wrong?"

"You look like you're about to give birth, Izela, except with no belly. Tell me what's going on. We can't have any surprises down here in the Crags."

6

The Day The  Helpless Fled

"If we had wings like the Crylia, this would be easy," Miasi said, slipping on her arse. She would have slid down the rest of the muddy slope if I hadn't grabbed her by the back of her dress and held. My other hand gripped a rock formation behind me, my palm scraping as I squeezed. My heart still pursued its pounding, and my body still flashed between icy cold and searing hot. But, I had work to do. I had to get my Queen safely through this harsh land.

"If we had wings like the Crylia," I grunted, pulling my Queen to her feet, "we'd be stuck underneath one of their males."

Once she found her footing, Miasi gripped my free hand and pulled me up beside her, chuckling. "You've already managed that, Iz."

"I don't feel very stuck, Mia. Believe me."

She brushed the mud from my face and frowned. "You do love him?"

"I...do. Very much."

"Has he earned it?"

"More than you could know...." I swiped at the perspiration beading on my forehead.

"Then...then we will have to marry you when this is all over." She nodded, her decision made. "A Tru wedding."

"Really, Miasi?"

"He may have earned your love, Izela. But you earned mine a long time ago." She put her hands on her hips, looking ahead to the long way we still had to travel. We were keeping low in the Crags, the fog giving us cover. But a wrong turn, and we'd be lost for months.

"I don't think I'll be a very good wife."

"You've always thought that."

"Well, I've been right so far. I'm a terrible mate. We've spent more time apart than together. Because of me."

"Just because you are complicated does not mean you aren't worth being pursued."

"I fear he'll be pursuing me all his days."

"Mm. Not to frighten you with my powers of Queenly perception, Izela but...you care to tell me what's wrong?"

"Wrong?"

"You look like you're about to give birth, Izela, except with no belly. Tell me what's going on. We can't have any surprises down here in the Crags."

I shook my head. "I don't know. Honestly. I feel...ill. But it's like no illness I've ever known. And no, I am not with child...."

"Are you certain?"

"I...would know." *I would know, wouldn't I? Of course I would.*

"How? Neither of us have been with child before. And who knows what your offspring would be like. What if...." Her voice grew quiet. "What if you laid an...an egg, Izzy."

"Gua bless me, you sound like my black wing. No. It feels like...the opposite of being with child. Empty. And...like my body is being pulled apart. Ruthlessly."

Her hands still on her hips, she glanced at me. "Well, I am thoroughly worried now."

"I am...concerned."

"You should have said earlier. We could have kept Maho with us."

"Mahopi cannot lead you through the Crags, Mia. He's too emotional, too wounded. Your judgment was right."

"Of course it was. I'm always right. And he may not have been able to lead, but Maho might have been able to carry you if your body gave out."

"I won't die here. Believe me." I started walking forward. "Of all the things my body is telling me, it screams loudest that I must not die. That I must find a way out of this nightmare and...." *Get back to my mate. Get back to him.*

"Which way? I thought it was left."

I groaned before I managed an answer. "It's to the right."

"How do you have such a good memory?"

"A spy needs to remember what she's seen, Miasi." *And what she's heard. And what she's done.*

She frowned at me. "I wish you could forget a few things, Iz. I really do."

"No time for apologies. No room for thanks."

"When will it be time? I haven't seen you in years—"

"You are my Queen. You can demand time if you wish." I was careful not to slip as I climbed over a fallen boulder, Miasi just behind me.

"I do not want to demand time. You're my friend. The closest thing I have to a sister. I want you to want to talk to me."

"We are talking now."

"About what happened, Iz."

"To the right." I changed the subject and hoped that Miasi would follow suit and change her mind. What was done was done. And going over the past would not bring us any closer. It certainly would not get either of us away from the invasion that had no doubt already begun behind us. "We need to get out of Tru territory before the Cryl take it all."

"Do not speak like that, Iz. Our people will survive. The Tru will always survive. Gua helps the helpless."

"*Tell me more....*"

I froze, reaching out and grabbing Miasi's arm. I gripped so hard I could have wrenched off her elbow.

The voice from behind us was cold and deep and slick, like a serpent bending its scales through slippery rocks.

"No, do go on. I have always been interested in this... *Helper*. This...Gua. But even more so, I have been interested in the helpless. The vulnerable. Those willing to do anything to avoid the sting of the powerful. To scrounge in the cracks. To...*beg*."

"Miasi," I whispered, my back still to Rizel Black Wing. "Run."

7

THE DAY THE  CRYL CHANGED

I meant for Miasi to run and hide, to make it through the Crags without me while I hurled myself forward to battle the black wing who'd found me, yet again, at my weakest point.

But I screamed in terror as my Queen shoved me aside and hurtled headlong toward our attacker. When she pushed me, I slipped, skidding down a steep incline with no indication as to the travesties unfolding above me except for the shout of a Tru gone mad and the rush of Crylia wings.

"Miasi!" I cried, clawing my way back up the side of the ravine, my fingernails tearing as I clutched sharp rocks to make my way to her. "Miasi!"

By the time I reached level ground again, Rizel had her. He had her. He had my Queen and oldest friend in his corded arms, his wings outstretched and flapping. But something came over me. It wasn't despair. It wasn't destitution. And it was nothing miraculous or dazzling. It was refusal.

I refused to let him take her.

So I picked up a stone and hurled it at him, aiming for his wing. I succeeded, sending him reeling to one side. I picked up another and threw with all my strength. With that, he went careening, colliding into the side of a stony spire. He released Miasi, but only to throw her behind him and to face me. She lay unmoving, only fueling my outrage.

"You want to fight me so badly, female?"

"Why not take me instead, Rizel? You wanted me before. In the snowy mountains of Led. So take me now. Leave her." *Leave my Queen alone.*

"My objective has been…amended."

I dug my heels into the dirt, trying to summon every bit of combat Nkita had ever taught me. It wasn't going to be enough. Nkita and I never seemed to have enough time….

"I won't let you take her!"

"No. You won't. You will end here. Beneath me."

I made a move, hoping to circle Rizel to get to Miasi, but I could not get past him. Not when he roared so loudly that it split my ears, that the Crags rumbled in fear. Not when he pounded his hands into the ground, bending his spine and assuming a menacing position on all fours, such that his clothes ripped and rent, his sword falling away and his eyes set on me. Fur no longer lined his skin in striations. No, it rippled along him in wild tufts, a tail whipping out from behind him. I looked not into the face of a Crylia as I knew them...but into the eyes of something different altogether.

A beast. A...monster. With fur and black feathered wings and talons, with eyes like a serpent and the razor-sharp beak of an eagle.

Perhaps I might have felt fear before, but this sort was new. It started at the soles of my feet and traveled up my body until every muscle trembled from within to without. *Gua...help the helpless.*

The beast was easily three times my size, still growing and heaving as it stood before me, it's bones cracking and creaking into place again and again.

It charged forward, and there was no time for me to run, no time for me to cower. Instead, I flew backward beneath its weight. It pinned me down with impenetrable talons, my ribs squeezed and groaning from the pressure of its grasp. I grabbed at fistfuls of hair on its massive forelegs, hoping to rip them away, hoping to cause the beast some pain before it devoured me.

With your Tru Queen and our Tonguekeeper...we will have everything we need. And I will have my rightful place restored at the Cza's side. I will drink and have my fill of females once more. I will be...Redeemed.

Drosya? Do...they have her? I struggled, waiting for the pain of death, inspiring a sort of maddening anticipation, an agony like nothing else. But Rizel did not kill me.

Instead, he hissed inside my mind, like a worm crawling through my thoughts. *It was an easy trade. Some useless blade for the likes of you. You were to lead me to that driveling coward, Opas. With him beneath my boot, I would win the Cza's approval once more. His head on a spike, his last pathetic wing unfurled like a banner as I returned to the Capital. But I never needed him, did I? I just needed you...to bring me her.*

I struggled, my bones threatening to splinter as he squeezed, but a realization began to awaken. The power of secrecy that had served me so well for so long. *He doesn't know I'm the Vessel. If he knew, he'd take me to the Cza. He doesn't know.*

Have you ever been taken by a fullform, muckeater? Of course not. You wouldn't survive—

I screamed at the thought of it, willing to thrash my bones to pieces if it meant I could get away.

But something sharp spun threw the air, grazing Rizel's throat. He roared, releasing me and turning to charge at his attacker, who led in all sword and no hesitation. Rizel swiped at him with a wide paw and sent the attacker skidding sideways.

With that opening, the monster swooped into the air.

More blades followed, chasing him as he flew. One sliced his wing, and the air grew heavy with a rageful cry.

Struggling to keep himself righted, Rizel disappeared over the tops of the Crags.

I forced myself to hurry to my feet, clutching my ribs and reaching for another rock as I faced my savior.

"Don't be like that, you pretty thing." The Cryl tossed long red hair from his eyes, his freckled face standing out against the gray stone and white fog as though he wore splatters of blood. Crimson eyes gleamed at me as he stuck out a long tongue. He kept his beautiful red wings untucked, adorning his armor.

"You *stay away* from me, Dagon," I croaked as loudly as I could, pain shooting through every limb. "*Stay away.*"

"That's no way to talk to an old friend, now is it?" Then, those red wing eyes shifted over to Miasi, who was just starting to wake. "And who do we have here?" He licked his lips. "A *treat*? For me? You shouldn't have."

8

The Day The Ropes Were Tied

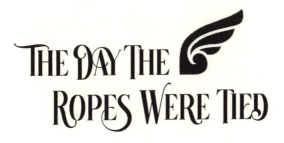

I scrambled to make sure I was between Dagon and Miasi as she struggled to wake.

"Protective of the sleepy one, are we?"

"Go ahead and fly away now, Dagon." I kept on the balls of my feet, even though my ribs shuddered and my stomach was being turned inside out from some force I did not understand. The dreadful sensation was even more alarming than the fact that I'd just witnessed a Crylia go from what I thought was a normal black wing to a four-legged beast the likes of which I'd never beheld.

"I thought you'd be happier to see me."

Miasi sat up, rubbing the back of her head. "What...what happened?"

"Mia, we need to get moving—"

"Why aren't you happier to see me? I am perplexed."

He chewed his bottom lip, looking me over slowly. "Usually females are ecstatic to be in my presence. They scream with excitement. We play a little chasing game. It's such fun."

"I'll be more excited to see you leave, Dagon."

"Who is *he*?" Miasi asked, standing behind me.

"I'm a friend," Dagon said, running his tongue over his lips as his red eyes darted around. "Speaking of friends, where is the old black wing General, anyway? Thought I'd find him romping around inside you for sure."

"He's getting us water."

"Ah, and Nkita Opas let Rizel Black Wing have his way with what's his while he was out filling a cute little basket?" Dagon pulled a blade from his belt and flipped it between his fingers. "So he's got to be pretty far off. Or...pretty occupied. Or both." He pointed the blade at me casually. "My bet is on both."

"*Listen—*"

"I was really hoping I could stab him back."

"Stab him back?" Miasi whispered, clearly concerned. "Stab *who* back?"

"It's my turn," Dagon whined.

"Why don't you go look for Nkita, then. He went that way—"

"I know he's not here. We've been over this." He narrowed his eyes. "But if I keep you, he'll come looking."

"No one will be keeping us." I raised my chin. "We're not objects."

"Sure." He nodded his head, scarlet eyes flashing. "Hold your hands out."

"I *won't*." I stepped backward as he came toward me.

"Hold your hands out, or I will lose my temper. I always get twitchy when I see someone else go fullform. Makes me want to have a little fun as well."

"Hold my hands out for what purpose?"

"I'm going to tie you up so you can't get away. Both of you. Nothing to worry about."

"I'm not—"

"He'll find you. Trust me. I found you quick enough. You're easier to track than he is. You smell strange."

I stumbled as we kept backing away, my body still shouting for me to stop moving.

"Black wings smell like nothing. Like air. And the still of death. But you? You smell like...."

Miasi gasped as our backs hit the stony wall of the cliff behind us.

"You smell like vengeance." Dagon was close enough to lean his hand against the wall behind me. He leaned in and inhaled deeply, the tip of his nose grazing the exposed skin beneath my collar bone. "Vengeance drives me mad," he explained.

"Touch me, Dagon, and I'll destroy you."

His eyes danced as he considered that. "It'd be an honor, little human. That is what you are, of course. Not a gold wing or a Grounded." He sniffed again. "I'm jealous. The General is so inventive. I wish I'd thought to take my own human prisoner."

Miasi bristled. "She's not—"

"Yes." I interrupted the Queen. "Yes, he has made me his mate and his prisoner. And he'll come for what belongs to him. So be careful with me, Dagon Red Wing."

I thought he'd listen. I'd thought he'd be frightened enough of Nkita's might that he'd back away from me, perhaps even let us escape. But instead, he reached out with incredible speed, grabbed one of my wrists, and pulled with a twist so that I was yanked from the wall, my shoulder nearly leaving its socket. He held me tight, my back against his chest, one hand gripping my hair, and the other pressing a rather sharp blade into the hollow beneath my jaw.

"You. Quiet one. Lie down on the ground."

I struggled to no avail. With every fraction I moved, Dagon pressed the blade further, until it pricked my skin and my blood found its escape down his forearm. I was not afforded the range of motion with which to speak, so I worked my hardest at evening my breath, at showing Miasi that I was calm and she should be too.

"Spread those arms out wide. Legs too," Dagon instructed her.

When she obeyed, he withdrew the blade from my throat only to shove me to my knees. He moved so quickly, I didn't have time to rise up or put up a fight. He wound a rope around my arms and torso, knotted it in less than a moment, and forced me all the way down to the ground. With my face on the rocky surface, he pressed his knee into the center of my back until I groaned, my ribs protesting under the strain.

"She's injured," Miasi said intuitively. "You're hurting her."

"A little pain makes things more interesting."

How many...ropes...does this Cryl...have? He fastened my wrists behind my back so tightly that I gasped. He then straightened himself out and dragged me over to Miasi, repeating his methodology on her. She didn't try to run. I knew she wouldn't. She would never leave me behind. That's not who my Queen was.

"If you hurt her—"

"The two of you are quite the pair," he said. I could hear that he was wearing a grin even if I couldn't see him.

"This is your grand plan, Dagon? To tie us up and wait until Nkita shows up to kill you?"

"No, no. That would be no fun at all. I'm going to drag you around Crylia. Make a little chase out of it. And when he does find you, Sweet Vengeance...I'll stab him back." Another rope. This time, he fastened it around my neck and one around Miasi's so he could lead us out of the Crags and into whatever random chaos lay ahead.

"Why? Dagon"—my words were cut short when he yanked me forward by the neck, and I stumbled over the loose stones, blinking through the fog.

"Don't be silly. It's good to make memories with friends."

9

The Day The Spy Called

"Izela," Miasi whispered as we stumbled through the Crags. "Izela, what's wrong?"

I wished she would pay more attention to her steps. With our hands tied behind our backs, it was a graceless fall anytime one of us tripped. And it didn't help that we were very obviously lost. "Focus, Miasi," I said through clenched teeth.

"Tell me what's wrong."

Besides being led through one of the most treacherous Tru terrains with a rope around my neck like I am chattel? I groaned as another wave of pain gripped my stomach, twisting my insides.

"Was it the black wing? Did he—?"

"No. No, Miasi." I understood her concern, but Rizel did little more than crack my ribs. That, and lead me to believe that the Cza had Drosya. And that for some reason, they needed Nkita. "Hush. Walk."

"You're in *pain*. Don't tell me to hush."

The pain, in fact, was increasing. Nearly debilitating. I wanted nothing more than to find Nkita Opas, to wrap my arms and legs around him, and to never leave him again. His heart slowing in his chest when mine beat out of control. The scent of him when I pressed my nose against his neck and drifted to sleep on his chest. *Gua, if you could shift the waters and bring us back together....*

"Keep up, friends!" Dagon called out in his sing-song voice. "We'll stop soon so I can feast on you—I mean so I can feast *with* you."

"Is he going to...*eat* us?" Miasi asked, her eyes wide, her gold and blue hair disheveled. "Do...red wings eat humans?"

"I...don't know...."

I stumbled on the rocks hidden beneath the fog and cracked my knees on the stony ground.

"Stop!" Miasi called out, resisting the pull of Dagon's rope. "Stop, you scarlet monster!"

"So dramatic," Dagon said, circling back to us. "I think I'll keep you when this is all through. Makes things more exciting to have a pet—I mean a friend."

"This isn't about your entertainment, red wing. Izela needs help, and I can't administer it with my hands tied behind my back. Release me."

"Who?" He scrunched his freckled nose. "I thought her name was Oahra—"

"It's not. She lied. She lied because I asked her to. Because I ask her to over and over. Her name is Emyri Izela, daughter of the Tru, and I need her to be alright. So untie me at once. She is clearly in distress—"

"Alright, alright. Let's just get through the Crags. Then we'll sort it."

"We can't make it through the Crags, red wing, because you are lost and she is on her knees!"

"I—I'm not lost! I know exactly where I'm going. Forward."

"You winged beasts are used to navigating from the air. You are hopeless on foot in a landscape like this. We Tru know the way. Let us help."

"Ha! I'm Crylia. I can find my way through anything. Besides, I don't do help. I do...."

"Madness? Wickedness?"

I chuckled despite my pain. I'd never heard Miasi so angry, never heard her words fly from her lips that quickly. I tried to intervene, to play peacemaker. "We... can quarrel...after we're out of here—"

Dagon sighed, wrapping the rope he used to lead us around his wrist and coming close to me. He put his hand on my jaw, looking into my eyes before turning my face this way and that.

"Speak again, pretty liar."

"Speak? And...say...what?" My voice was hoarse and shaking as I knelt. My entire body shivered with tremors, in fact.

"You are Calling for him."

"Wh-what?"

"Your mate, you fool. You're making a Call."

Miasi squirmed, kneeling beside me. "Untie me so I can help her—"

"She doesn't need help," Dagon said, his face hardening. "All she needs to do is stop *wanting* him and she'll be fine. We still have some distance to go."

"D-distance?" I wanted to lie all the way down, to curl up and let the pain take over.

"You parted with your mate but you want him. So your body Calls to his. It's very simple."

Miasi shook her head. "That doesn't cause illness. She's been apart from him before, and this did not happen. Isn't that so, Iz?"

"I...." I didn't want him to find me then. I thought he would be better off. I thought he would live a longer, better life if he wasn't with me. *But this time...I'm afraid for him. I'm afraid he won't make it back to me. Just like I was when he left me at the Cza's command.*

"Much like a birth tether. The tighter the bond, the stronger the Call," Dagon grumbled. "But at least it means the General will be coming to play soon." He tugged on our leads so that we had no choice but to find our footing and follow. "Better get to where we need to be before he shows."

"Must you be so cruel?" Miasi growled.

"She won't *die* from the Call," Dagon said with a scoff. "Not this soon, at least. Besides, cruelty is the best part of any game."

"Tell us where you think we are going," Miasi said, worry shining in her eyes when she glanced at me.

"It's not very fun if you don't know, I suppose." He yanked on the ropes once more for good measure and to keep us on pace. "We're off to see your enemies. My...employers. After my feast, of course. For that bit, we'll stop at the doubling tree." He chuckled. "Won't be long now. I'm famished."

10

The Day The  Slaver Flew

"I can't settle down unless you shut your knobsucker," Dagon growled from across the light of the low fire he'd lit.

"She's praying," I said.

"She's riling my feathers is what she's doing."

"Leave her alone." I stretched my foot out, trying to kick his boot but I couldn't reach. Something about being tied to a rocky spire made it impossible for me to do much of anything.

"How long does it last? The mumbling?"

"As long as Gua requires. Now leave her alone."

We needed Miasi's prayers now more than ever. I couldn't tell what was happening to the people we'd left behind—the old ones and the young, the fishermen and farmers, the sheepherders and basket weavers who'd lived simple lives for a thousand years. Their world was being crushed by countless Cryl warriors. *Searching for Nkita? For the Tonguekeeper? For Miasi?*

Searching for...me?

"I need to sleep," Dagon complained. I get...wild...if I don't."

"You're already *wild*."

He grinned through the hazy smoke. "Thank you."

I sighed. "These restraints aren't necessary, Dagon. Release me. As you've said, we're friends."

He sharpened his blade and peered at me over the flames. "You won't even stay put for the General, Goldie. I'm not chancing it. You're a runner if ever I saw one."

"Then...at least tell me where we're going. Please."

"To see the enemy. I told you."

"Which enemy? Whose enemy? The...the Hresh?"

"I don't bargain with Hresh." He spit on the ground to make his point. Then he paused, as if reminiscing. "I did like tying up that one in my cabin, though."

"You don't bargain with Hresh. But, you work for the Cza? Like...like Nkita did?"

"I'm not Teth if that's what you mean. Czas don't tether to red wings. In fact, most Generals won't even let red wings join their ranks. Those that do enlist us as berserkers."

"Is that what you did for Nkita?"

"No. No, he enlisted me for other...reasons. Only General who would."

"But...why?" *Get him talking. Keep him talking. Learn what you can. And lie.* The tenets of a good spy. "What's wrong with red wings?"

"Nothing is wrong with us! They claim we're 'unpredictable' at best and 'absolutely mad' at worst." He shrugged. "Fine with me. I refuse to be tethered to some white wing, tasked to keep him preened and pretentious all his days. Don't know how Opas can stand it."

"At least he's free now...."

Dagon glanced up at me. "Free? Free how?"

"No longer a Grand Teth."

Dagon clicked his tongue. "Oh no, pretty liar. That's not how it works."

"Nkita said he's no longer—"

"He can say he's not Grand Teth all he wants. But unless the Cza is dead or Nkita is dead, they're tethered. From birth to now. Maybe he doesn't serve like a Teth serves, but—"

"The Cza—"

"*Never* cuts a tether. Not even if he Cages someone. Or Grounds them. Not even if he fells them—"

"*No one* is felling my mate," I snapped.

He looked me over and bit his lip. "Missing him that bad, hm?"

I sucked air in through my teeth. "It...*hurts*."

"Hurts for him worse, I bet."

"Worse?"

"He is more yours than you are his. That much is clear."

"How is that—?"

"I bet, Goldie, he's out there right now doing some twisted, messy shite for you. And what are you doing for him, hm? Chatting with Dag? Sleeping with Da—"

"No."

"I am very good."

"No."

"Not like those white wing males that force their mates to lie still and whimper—"

"Dagon Red Wing. *No*."

He sighed. "Fine. Another time."

"No other time. Never."

He nodded his head toward Miasi, who had her eyes closed and her head tilted up as she lifted the prayers of her people to Gua. "What about her?" He licked his lips. "She has *chaos* to her."

"Hands off my Queen, red wing."

"She might *want* my hands on her. You haven't even asked."

"The day my Miasi allows you to touch her is the day"—a rush of air. The unmistakable sound of wings moving the currents around us, chasing the fog and reducing the fire to mere embers.

"Finally," Dagon said, rising to his feet. "You take the troublemaker. I'll take the mumbling one."

A large Cryl with white wings so filthy and beaten they might as well have been gray. He grunted as he moved toward me.

"I...I *know* you...." I squirmed away, sliding back as far as I could, the jagged stone pressed against my spine. "You saved my life. And...." *And Drosya's.* I swallowed, utterly confused. "Take us...take us where?"

"You?" Cyndr the slaver pointed a meaty finger at me. "Why are you not with the Pureblood Heir? What was the point of saving you from the slavers if you are not with him, keeping his nest warm?"

"Save your lectures for later, rebel," Dagon chided. "I have sleep to catch. Up with them, already."

Cyndr growled as he untied me and grabbed me by the arm, pulling me to my feet. But I was more concerned with Miasi than I was for myself.

"Let her finish the prayers, Dagon. *Dagon*! Let her—"

But he grabbed Miasi and wrapped his arms around her, shooting off into the air.

"Prayers?" Cyndr asked. "What are prayers?"

"She's speaking with Gua—"

"Who's *Gua*? Is there another of you? I can only carry one at a time—"

"She's here but not here. She's the goddess of w—"

Cyndr did not wait for me to explain who the goddess was or how patiently she blessed both our land and theirs, about how she kept the Tru land warm and our rivers flowing. Instead, he propelled us upward into the air, his thick forearms crushing my already injured ribs as he held me fast.

Flying with Cyndr was nothing like flying with my black wing. Nkita...he flew with grace and precision, as if the air were made for him and he for it.

But Cyndr made smaller movements with his wings despite his girth and weight. His white wing way of flying resulted in us making worse time than Dagon, who flew like there were bees in his trousers. Miasi must have been through with her prayers because she screamed every time the red wing swooped and turned.

The air above the Crags was too warm, as if the heat of the day had been caught in an invisible net hovering over the stones and fog. And from that high up, I could smell the smoke from behind us. I was certain I could see the ash settling on Tru land if only I could turn my head. For a moment, I swore I could hear the screams of innocent humans as the Crylia rained terror down on them. Even Miasi grew quiet. I knew, once again, she was praying, for I prayed too. Not for ourselves. But for the people she served and the people I loved, even when they did not love me.

Gua. Help the helpless.

11

The Day The Prisoners Landed

We flew until day broke and a circle of tents and lean to's greeted us from below. The makeshift settlement was nestled in a shallow valley to the north, not quite as far as Led but not quite as close as Yogdn. Once we made landfall, we were surrounded by a ragged crew of what appeared to be mercenaries, for they wore no uniforms, only the shoddiest of armor protecting their bodies. Just bloodied shirts and muddied boots. Most wore a pair of wings.

And every single one of them had weapons trained on Miasi and me.

Hrogar Gray Wing stepped forward, his one-eyed face scrunched into a scarred scowl. "Get far from here now, red wing. We're through with you."

Dagon scoffed, tugging Miasi back toward himself by the hair so she was firm against his chest. "I stay." He tilted his head. "I'm waiting for a friend."

"You did what we asked. Tracked the Queen and the gold wing. Now it's time for us to part ways." Hrogar hurled a sack of coin at Dagon, who allowed the sack to strike his shoulder and the gold to spill to the soggy ground.

"I stay."

"Then we have a problem—"

"Let the red wing merc stay," someone said, parting the weapon-wielding Crylia and nodding at me. "Cyndr, let her go. She is, after all, our Future Queen."

I knew her as well. Rhaza. The little Grounded who saved us when the Cza had us trapped. I owed her my life and I was immensely relieved and equally stressed to see her here.

Cyndr grunted. I almost forgot the giant still had me in his grasp. Whether he intended to harm me or not, I felt safer with Cyndr than I expected.

I smoothed my dress and pointed to Miasi. "The...the human Queen is under my protection." A quick pivot. *These Crylia rebels still believe I'm a Grounded gold wing, mate of the Pureblood Heir.* I glanced at Dag to see if he would keep my secret. Unpredictable. That's what Cryl called red wings. Would he help me or harm me?

"Release the prisoner if the Queen wishes it," Rhaza said. "Keep a close eye on her. It is no secret the Tru and the Crylia are not friendly." She set steely gray eyes on Miasi. "But, to be clear, we rebels have no quarrel with the Tru. Ours is with the tyrant Cza who sits on the throne and steals our offspring, making them his Teth."

"I thought...the nobles volunteer their offspring," I said.

"As if they would do so willingly. Some do. Many do not."

What of Nkita's parents? Had they chosen to bind their offspring to the Cza, or was it forced? The Cza had forced Nkita and me to wed. Perhaps he was not the first in his line to have his choices taken from him.

I raised my chin and tried to pretend I was queenly. "Why have we been brought here?"

"Very simple," Rhaza said. "We want the Pureblood Heir. *Krov vanya crystin*. He must lead us to victory and sit upon the throne."

"You think he will be amenable to you after you've mistreated me and those under my protection?"

Rhaza shot a look at Dagon and spoke through gritted teeth. "You have been mistreated?" She crossed her arms. The threat in her eyes was clear.

What happened to the frail, sweet gray wing I'd met on the steps of the Castle? Seemed I was not the only spy in the Capital, for the Crylia female before me was not feeble in the least. She was commanding and stern, but her tone was steeped in understanding.

"I was perfectly lovely," Dagon said with a frown. "Ask. She'll tell you."

"Dagon was...Dagon."

"Thank you."

"I am being held here against my will," I explained to Rhaza. "That is mistreatment enough."

"We will hope the true Cza is just and understanding." She sighed. "We will make you comfortable until he arrives."

"She's been Calling—"

"Dagon!" I blushed.

"He'll be here soon. Unless he's dead."

"Bite your tongue, you bloodplucked fool," Hrogar said, raising his blade.

"No more fighting," Rhaza said, her hand up. "Cyndr is hungry enough to bite all our heads off." She waved. "Go and eat. All of you." Then to me, she bowed her head. "Queen of the Cryl, you and your prisoner will both be shown to your quarters. No one will harm you. I give you my word."

I paid close attention as the rebels scattered, back to their tasks, their weapons sheathed. I studied the paths we took as we moved through the campground, surveyed the faces of those around me. Who were spies? Who were loyal to the Cza? Who were fanatics bent on forcing Nkita to take a crown he did not want?

And most importantly...*where do the routes through the campground lead?* The sooner Miasi and I could take our leaves, the better. Nkita would find me. This, we all knew. But, so help me Gua, he wouldn't find me here.

Immediately, Miasi and I were separated. It was clever of them. There was no way I'd leave without her, and they must have known that. Being apart from her made everything far more complicated.

Once my guard and I made it to the humblest of tents—and truly all of them were humble—Cyndr put a burly hand on my shoulder and lowered me to the floor. I resisted, but not for long. The Cryl was strong.

"I'll need your ankle, Queen."

"My...my what?" I looked up at him from on my knees, my hands still tied behind my back, my stomach still writhing in pain. *What is this?*

"I apologize. But...I have my orders. I must ensure you do not escape. Both the red wing and Hrogar One Eye said you are skilled at disappearing."

I narrowed my eyes and set my resolve. "I am not going to let you shackle me, Cyndr. I warn you. I will fight. And you will have the dishonor of harming me. Are you prepared for that?"

"If you would just"—he bent over and reached for the hem of my dress.

12

THE DAY THE SPY HEARD

Cyndr sighed and backed away when I kicked at him.

"Let me just—"

"You will have to hurt me to get it done. I am through with being tied up and dragged around all of Miror. I am not chattel. I am—" *I almost said a human being. But that would give me away.* "I am a Crylia. Same as you. I won't be bound."

"One would think a Grounded was used to being forced."

"What is the big difference?! Between you and a Grounded?"

Cyndr balked at that, clearly confused that such a question could ever be formed, much less posed to him by someone like me.

"Perhaps...you do have the makings of a queen. Perhaps the future Cza was right to choose—"

A gruff voice inserted itself into the tent. "What is the big hold up here, Cyndr?"

"I can't, Hrogar." The big Cryl frowned, his shoulders slumping. "She won't let me."

Hrogar scoffed, shoving past the white wing. "What sort of slaver are you if you can't tie up a Grounded female?"

"I can do it, Hrogar. I just...she won't let me."

"Pin her down and take her over! She's not your Queen *yet*, fool. Give me that." He snatched the rope from Cyndr's hands. "I know her for what she is, you see. Spent enough time hiding her and the black wing. She's a slippery little serpent of a female who never does as she's told and never stays where she's put. A real muckeater."

"*Hrogar—*"

"If you don't want to see me tie her up like a hog for sale, then get out."

"I won't—"

"Get out, Slaver. Go coddle Rhaza while she pretends to lead us. Go. Or I'll have you Caged along with the other dissenters."

Cyndr reached out and grabbed the rope back from Hrogar. "What *happened* to you, One Eye? You didn't used to be so—"

"Honest?"

"I was going to say shite-mouthed."

"I used to be a soft one. Like you. But soft ones aren't worth the air they breathe. Learned that the hard way. Now give that rope back."

"I'll secure her myself." And the tone in Cyndr's voice changed so that no one, not even Hrogar, would question him. Once the mean old Cryl was gone, Cyndr looked me in the eye. "Rhaza tells me you are called Syiva."

Of course. That was the name I used when the Cza had me imprisoned in his castle. Keep all identities straight. Remember not only who you're pretending to be now, but you pretended to be at any given time. "Yes."

"Well, Syiva…here is the thing. We rebels are not the sort to let our cause fade away. We are zealous to be finished with this tyrant Cza. And so, in their zeal, others may become…forceful. But I do not want to force you. I believe you are important to our future Cza. And I want his favor to fall on me, not his vengeance."

"This is a long speech, white wing."

"All of it is to say this. I once showed kindness to you. Took you from enslavement and set you free. What I am asking now, is that you trust me once more. I will let no harm come to you. But I would rather it be I who makes sure you cannot flee."

"This is a kindness you show me? To shackle me once more?"

"No, my queen. This will be a kindness you show me."

I inhaled, straightening my shoulders. "Listen well, Cyndr. If Nkita Opas finds out you restrained me, no matter who traded kindness to whom, he will rain down judgment. So…here is the kindness I'll show. You leave me be, no restraints, and I give you my word I will not run until he comes."

"…Truly?"

"Truly."

Cyndr nodded and tossed me the rope in his rough way. "Here then. Tie these around your ankles in case anyone comes to check. You will seem to be restrained, but will have your freedom to move about."

"Good. And thank you."

"Thank *you*, Queen Syiva."

As soon as he left, I began to look around. *Foolish Cryl. My word means nothing.* He had not yet learned he should never trust a spy.

And spy I would. Finding my Tru Queen and escaping the rebel camp would not be good enough. I wanted to know everything they were planning, everything they were hiding. What they considered their objectives, their strengths. And what they could not see as weaknesses. I would gather all this information, and it would make me valuable to anyone who opposed me or the ones I loved.

I found I could slip beneath one of the loose corners of the tent if I crawled out on my belly. I did so, fighting the pain and fueled by the energy I needed to do what I had to do. I found myself in a dark space, the light blocked perhaps by cloths over the cutout windows.

This would have been perfectly fine if not for the blood-chilling sounds that seeped through to this area. Grunts and hisses and the sound of blows hitting flesh and bone.

I froze, listening, trying to will my eyes to adjust to the dark. I realized nothing and no one was in this empty part of the tent. Whatever was making those sounds, they were not immediately present. But when I crawled forward, when I made my limbs move, I came closer and closer to the terrifying source of the noise.

At last, I put my hand on the canvas on the other side of the room. All I had to do was move the hem of that partition up, just a hair, with my nose to the ground. Then, with luck, I would see who or what was being beaten to death.

What are these rebels doing? And to whom? And how does a little Tru spy with no armor and no weapons and no army...put a stop to it?

13

THE DAY THE CRYL BLED

With my belly to the ground and my cheek pressed to the dry dirt, I slipped my fingers beneath the hem of the canvas and peered into the partition. It was dark, but I could still make out everyone present.

Hrogar, of course. Wherever he was, good things died. And there were other Cryl I'd seen when we arrived. Hanging from a pole in the center of the tent, wrists bound and lifted over his head, was Dagon Red Wing. His armor was gone, his bare chest revealed as he took blow after blow from the Crylia rebels.

Mostly, he groaned in response. But, after a particularly vicious blow to the stomach, he rocked his head forward, red hair covering his swollen face, and laughed.

"He's mad," Hrogar said, spitting on the ground. "But what else could we expect?"

My stomach clenched at the sight of Dagon being beaten this way. Yes, the Cryl had been nothing but trouble for me, for Miasi, for Nkita. But still, he did not deserve to be tortured for it. My head pounded as I tried to comprehend, to understand why these rebel Cryl would do what they were doing? Dagon had brought Miasi and I to him, just as he was meant to. *What is the point of bludgeoning him this way?*

I would learn the truth if I was still, if I was silent and patient. I'd learned so many things that way already. And I had paid for the knowledge I'd gained in more ways than anyone would ever know.

But now, I could do some good with it.

"It's time you told us, red wing, unless you want to die here hanging from this tent." Hrogar nodded, and the rebel Cryl smashed his fist upward into Dagon's face once more. "All we need is a location."

And all Dagon did…was laugh.

"I want you to know, we will do what we must to find them." Hrogar signaled for Dag to be struck once more. "We need this information and we are confident a rogue like you has heard tell. That you know where they are." Another blow, one that had to have cracked Dagon's skull. "We want the Vessels. All three."

The Vessels? Certainly, these rebels did not know I was most likely one of them. Neither did they know I was the last of the three. And lucky for me, neither did Dagon.

But they did not believe he had no idea, which meant they would beat this red wing to death on the hunt for someone he'd unknowingly brought to them already.

I had other questions. What did the rebels want with the Vessels? And why did they think Dag knew where the Vessels were?

I stood back up, deciding to return to the room that was supposed to be my prison before I was caught and strung up and beaten. But the moment I turned around, I rammed right into the broad chest of Cyndr.

"Oh," I said, clearing my throat and scrambling for a story that would cover my tracks. "I was just looking for a way to relieve mys—"

"You *lied* to me."

"I was just going back—"

"You are *escaping*."

"I'm not escaping. I heard screams—"

"I should have tied you up."

"Why would I have been on the ground looking through to the next tent if I was trying to run away, Cyndr? Think about this."

"I don't know, but—"

"Why are you beating the red wing who brought me here?" *Change the subject. Catch him off guard.*

Cyndr narrowed his eyes at me. "You're defending him? We brought you here against your will."

"I don't want to see him killed, even if he is terrible."

Cyndr scowled. "Honestly? Rhaza is not one for beatings. I...am surprised she is allowing it."

Ah. An opportunity. "Perhaps she does not know."

"No one would do such a thing without her ordering it."

"Let's ask her, Cyndr." I winced at the sound of another blow from behind me. "It wouldn't hurt to ask."

"Fine," he said, cracking his large neck. "But you're coming with me. Where I can keep an eye on you."

I nodded. "Let's go talk to Rhaza." That way I could get a good look at the campground, find the exits, the points of danger. Find Miasi. And then get far, far away. But...Dagon....

I couldn't just leave him to die, could I? Nkita had already done so once. I presumed the red wing dead already. Perhaps this was his fate. I shook my head as Cyndr led me through the camp. No. No, I couldn't just leave Dag. I had to try.

Into the main tent we went and found Miasi sitting very comfortably on the ground. Rhaza addressed her rebels, her posture relaxed and confident, her armor chipped and worn and ill-fitting, as if it had belonged to someone else before her. She wore her Grounded ring in her lip and her gray hair she kept in a braid down her back.

"Rhaza," Cyndr said as we approached.

Miasi sighed with relief at the sight of me. She mouthed to me in Tru, asking if I was alright. I nodded my head and mouthed back the same.

"You have needs, Queen Syiva?" Rhaza asked, pausing her meeting. "I assure you we have kept your Tru prisoner comfortable."

"Rhaza, I owe you my life. Mine and my mate's. You saved us from the Cza's castle. And you sent us to Hrogar to keep us safe in the woodlands."

"I wish I could have done more. And sooner. We might have spared the Pureblood Heir his wing and his dignity."

I wanted to say that Nkita's dignity was fully intact, but that was not going to be helpful. I needed to be clever. To...manipulate. It was a subtle art. "I want you to know that I forgive you." I held my breath, hoping I was playing her correctly. I wasn't sure whether to appeal to Rhaza's compassion or to her pride. So I went with the latter.

"Forgive me? I'm afraid I don't understand."

"For what you're doing to the red wing who helped you."

Rhaza scrunched her brow. "Explain."

"I mean...how your Cryl are beating him to death right now. I could hear it from my tent and I know you must have given the order—"

"Show me where," Rhaza said, her expression hardening. She glared at Cyndr. "You didn't come to me with this?"

"I've just learned of it and brought Syiva to you—"

"You should have stopped them," Rhaza barked. She began walking, expecting us to follow. "Who?"

"Hrogar One Eye," Cyndr said, taking long steps in order not to fall behind.

"Keep up," Rhaza said as she neared the tent where Dagon was being kept. "Not only is this the last time Hrogar defies my orders, it's the last time he'll draw breath."

14

The Day The Spy Fell In Line

Rhaza made it three more steps before rebels left Hrogar's tent and came at us, weapons in hand.

"You bloodplucking traitors," she said between gritted teeth. "What do you think you are doing?"

"Hrogar says you are too mild. A female leading us? And a Grounded at that? What more could we expect?" one rebel said, an axe in hand as he faced us.

"And you all feel this way?" Rhaza asked, raising her voice and catching the attention of everyone in the camp. "You all feel a female—a Grounded female—is not fit to lead you until our Pureblood Heir arrives? Hm?"

Half of the camp stepped over to Rhaza. The other half sided with Hrogar, just as he stepped out of the tent, using a rag to wipe Dagon's blood from his knuckles. "I see it is time you faced the truth, Rhaza. A Grounded female? Pretending to lead? And a Grounded female who will take the place of our Queen?"

He began a rambling tirade, during which I shot a look at Miasi and then darted my eyes toward the tent behind Hrogar. She gave a subtle nod, understanding what I was signaling, and then slowly, quietly tiptoed away from the standoff, circling around the crowd that had gathered.

No one thought Miasi was a threat. They hadn't bound her hands or feet. She was free to slip into Dagon Red Wing's tent undetected while I bore the brunt of Hrogar's insults at Rhaza's side.

It took quite a while for anyone to realize their prisoners were missing. A few shouts let Hrogar know he'd failed his attempt at a coup. The brawling began next, rebels against mutineers. Rhaza's first priority was to step between the rabble and me, taking a blade to the shoulder as she did so.

I wrapped my arms around her middle and pulled her backward until I could go no further.

"Let me go!" she said, wriggling away from my grasp. Heaving, she knelt in the dirt, her face paling as blood left her wound. "To those hills," she said, pointing behind me. "We hide there."

"Let me carry you," I told her. She had no wings to propel us through the air. Even if she did, I would be too heavy for her, and she couldn't use Old Cryl to make it happen like Umra had when we once escaped through a tavern window. "I can hold you on my back."

"You can't—"

"There is no time and I won't leave you behind."

I moved up to Rhaza and hoisted her onto my back. Working as a servant and then running for my life through the woodlands of Crylia had made me stronger than I ever thought possible. I was able to make decent time with the rather lightweight female. When I was too tired to go further, I stalled, my hand on a tree trunk while I caught my breath.

I gasped as someone came from behind us and took Rhaza from me.

"Cyndr!" I cried.

"I found your friends," he said. "This way." And he began moving, carrying Rhaza with him. He had her tossed over his shoulder like she was a sheep he'd saved from a briar patch.

Should I trust the Cryl? Or is he leading me straight into danger?

I was about to take a step forward, to follow him into peril only Gua knew, when someone clamped a hand over my mouth and pulled me back into the trees.

I would have fought. I would have fought for my very life. But when those hands touched my body, I felt nothing but the most intense mixture of relief and desire I'd ever endured. I ought to have been ashamed by the whimper I let out as I melted backward into his chest.

He turned me around, holding me to him, and I wrapped my arms around his middle and tried not to lose my mind as I breathed him in. I didn't realize I was weeping until he lifted my chin and kissed me. His lips were cool against mine, his tongue warm as it entered my mouth, moving in slow circles...soothing me.

With his thumbs he swiped at my tears as he pulled away. "Are you hurt, Em?"

I shook my head. Everything in my body that ached, that stung and twisted and convulsed due to his absence quieted. Then it roared to life once more.

I kissed my mate as if fire consumed me and he was the deepest river, chills washing over my being like ripples. His hands met my waist, and I knew he wanted to tear my dress from my body. To press me to the forest floor and greet me properly. But we were in a crisis. And there was no time.

"Tell me what happened."

"Rebels," I said, still keeping my hips pressed to him, just so I could feel close. "They used Dagon to find us. To find you. But Hrogar...he formed a mutiny."

"They're after you?"

I nodded. "The camp is down that hill."

"We must go. Get you safe—"

"No!" I gripped his armored shoulder. "Nkita, we can't leave Miasi. Rhaza, Dagon...."

"*You* are my first priority. Always. I will come back for them when you are safe—"

"We bring them with us."

"Emyri—"

"We're not leaving them for Hrogar to find. I won't do it."

My mate put those lavender eyes on me, and I noticed for the first time the fresh wounds and bruises he wore on his stern face. I wanted to know what he'd battled to make it back to me. But that too would have to wait.

I wouldn't leave my Queen behind. And the General knew it.

He sighed. "Fine. But if we slow down for them"—he took my jaw in his grasp, squeezing just enough and tilting my head up so I had to look into those eyes. "You. Will. Do. As. I. Say."

I swallowed, biting my lip and surprised to find I still had no Grounded ring there.

"I need to hear it, Em."

I groaned. "Yes."

"Yes?" He squeezed just a bit harder.

I tried not to lose my composure. "Yes...First General Grand Teth Nkita Opas of the Cza's Army...sir."

He let go of me and grabbed my wrist, leading me forward. But I noticed he wore the tiniest smirk before I fell in line behind him.

15

The Day The Spy Faced The Soldier

I want to stop him. I want to slide my hands up his neck and lean into his kiss. I want to dig my nails into his skin, tangle my fingers into his hair—

"Why must you keep falling behind, Em? Are your human legs so frail?"

"You like the strength of these human legs just fine," I snapped.

"We need to move qui—"

"I am *walking*, Nkita. This is as fast as I go."

I knew he tensed from the tug I felt in my own muscles. He fell quiet, searching in the woods for where my friend might have gone.

I am being mean. No...I am being angry. Why? He hasn't done anything to deserve it. I attempted to bring myself calm by taking deep breaths and admiring the clouds Gua was spinning into the sky as the gray floated through the tree leaves above me. *Calm, Em.*

Calm. Be good to him. "How...how did it go? Did the Crylia—" *Did they destroy everything I loved?*

"Many were lost."

My heart began to thud in my chest. This was not helping me stay calm, not helping me quell the storm in my body.

"Some were saved," he continued.

I caught up to him and grabbed his arm, slowing him down for a moment. "Nkita, *thank you*."

"No need for thanks."

"You're wrong. There is *much* need for thanks. You risked your life to save my people."

"No." His eyes were stern. "I risked my life for *you*."

The breath was sucked from my lungs as I stared back into his eyes. He meant it. He'd always meant it. And maybe he always would. "All the more reason to thank you." *I could show him. I could show him right now—*

"We move."

I bit back my groan of frustration as we kept on. The twisting, burning pain of being apart from the black wing was replaced by a deep, clawing ache to be even closer. *What part of being mates with a Cryl is supposed to be pleasant?*

More crashing through the brush for us. Nkita's steps were quick and sturdy, like a black wing's, I assumed. I'd seen gray wings plod through the forest, and they were not as expedient as Nkita. I, as well, was not so quick but I was precise. Tru were good at being invisible, and we'd practiced the art of silent walking out of necessity. Nkita walked the forest like a hunter. I walked through the forest like prey.

"I think they're just ahe—"

Like a stone from the sky, something or someone dropped from the tree branches above us, kicking me to the side and falling onto Nkita's back. I was too startled to scream, and when I finally focused my eyes, I realized that it was indeed a 'someone', and that someone had crimson hair and matching freckles. He also held a blade in his hand. From the way Nkita roared, Dag had run that blade into the top of the shoulder of my black wing.

Nkita spun, throwing the red wing off his back and turning to face him, long sword drawn.

"Found you," Dag purred, his red eyes wide and his tongue curling up over his top lip. It was clear he'd been beaten badly, his face swollen and bleeding among his cheekbone and the ridge of his forehead. "Owed you one."

Nkita charged but Dag zoomed upward, his wings giving him an advantage Nkita would have negated if not for me. Dagon perched on a branch, looking more like a bird than I'd seen any Cryl look, and growled, his cheer vanishing. "I'm going to watch you bleed to death and then take your mate back to my cabin with her little regal one. Two humans for the red wing."

I shivered at the tone his voice took. Dark and cold and inky, like ice forming over black waters.

I wasn't sure what to do, what to say. And I wasn't really afraid until Nkita dropped his sword, gripping his injured arm.

"Emyri," he said through gritted teeth. And then he spoke to me in Tru, his tongue a little stiff over some of the consonant sounds from too many years of speaking Cryl. But still...he spoke to me in Tru, the words of my people leaving his lips and meeting my ears. "Go find the Queen...and run north. I'll find you."

I closed my eyes, my heart racing not because Nkita was in danger, not because just maybe this mad red wing had truly injured him in a way I could not understand... but because I would have to leave him again. And that would hurt every bone in my body. I was tired of missing him. Tired of running *from* the one I loved instead of *to* him.

So, I did not do as he said. My body simply couldn't take being apart from him any more.

Instead, I walked forward at a slow pace, lifted his sword from the ground, and pointed it at Dagon.

"You won't be taking me anywhere, red wing," I said, keeping my voice even. Calm flooded my body, as if Gua herself was pouring peace and power over me. "There is only one person who will regret the choices you made, and it's you."

Dagon tilted his head, his red eyes dilating so that his irises were the thinnest slivers. His wings were beautiful scarlet and gold as the feathers spread around his shoulders. A flash through my memory of the terrifying form Rizel took when he tried to capture me in the Crags. Could Dagon do that as well? And more importantly... would he?

"You want to play, Tru? Your pretty friend told me you like games before I strung her up in that tree."

Stay calm. Stay calm, Em.

"Emyri—" Nkita tried.

"*I'm not leaving you,*" I said more loudly than I planned. I stood between him and the red wing and had every intention of dying there if need be. *I've lost enough. You won't become one of my memories. Not you.*

But Nkita Opas stepped forward and wrapped his arm around me, pulling me back to his chest and kissing my neck while I kept my eyes trained on Dagon.

"Fine," he said, his voice raspy against my temple. "We can fight him. But you'll do as I say."

I inhaled as he slid his hand down to my wrist, tightening my grip on the sword for me. It was incredibly heavy for me to hold, and his added strength was appreciated.

"How endearing," Dagon muttered, still studying us from his perch, his talons sprouting from his fingers and clawing at the branch that held his weight.

"I'll need to hear it, Em," Nkita said. It worried me that his voice sounded quieter in my ear.

I braced myself as Dagon began beating his wings, prepared to descend. "Yes...First General Grand Teth Nkita Opas of the Cza's Army...sir."

16

The Day The  Two Became One

Nkita whispered one more thing in my ear. "*Por nus-ya gohori.*"

His words sizzled down my spine, and something fierce flowed through me, threatening to crack my bones. It didn't help that my mate let go of my wrist, returning his hand to my stomach and fortifying my core so I leaned back against him once more. "Go on," he said to me.

Dagon landed on the ground, drawing his own blade and walking a slow circle around us. We turned as he did, and I'd never felt more like prey in my life.

But Nkita's hand was strong against my center, and I exhaled.

"Em. Go on."

Go on? Does he mean I should attack? Or...or run?

"*Por nus-ya gohori*," he said one last time.

A buzz on my lips, and a dizzy smell that clouded my vision. My head throbbed, and I nearly dropped the blade. But then, the words wiggled themselves to my mouth and rolled off my tongue, shattering the pain they caused me. "*Por…nus-ya…gohori.*"

There came more of that strength, that power, that… pure chaos. It was unstable, wrecking my body as it pulsed and coursed. I struggled not only to hold the sword, but to breathe. And with Dagon making his move, his blade high and coming down on us, his nostrils flared and his wings giving him more speed than I could fathom, I screamed out.

I raised the sword to protect myself. Nkita helped me, his arm lifting mine. But Dagon came at me with such strength that my boots skidded backward in the damp soil. If not for Nkita's firm stance supporting me, I would have gone flying, my body colliding with the nearest tree.

With a roar, I shoved Dagon and his blade back, the sound of our metal swords grinding against each other sending a spark of excitement through me I didn't expect.

"I'm surprised," Dagon said, licking his lips. "I love surprises." He tossed his head like a bear about to swat a fish out of the river. "You'll be surprising between my legs too, I bet. I've had a human once or twice." He chuckled. "They're…loud."

"Steady," Nkita whispered in my ear. "You are strength, Emyri. Strength is steady. *Por nus-ya gohori.*"

"*Por nus-ya gohori,*" I said with a bit more confidence. I didn't know what the Old Cryl words meant but I knew they were doing something to me. They held some secret my mind hadn't yet unlocked. But Nkita knew. *How...how does Nkita know? What has he not told me?*

"Pay attention—"

Dagon struck again. This time, he came in lower and at an angle, his sword aiming for my heart. I took three fast steps back, and it must have been the right thing to do because Nkita moved with me. We ducked, sidestepped, and took two long steps forward to strike. *These motions...*I'd just begun to learn them back in the foundry in the Capital when Nkita thought it best to teach me a lesson or two. But this was so different. Moving in the heat of the moment required instinct and fearlessness.

Dagon blocked my attack and let out a loud burst of laughter. "She strikes back! What a match you made, hm, old friend?"

Nkita stepped me backward and then put his hand up to my chin, lifting it higher. "Eyes up, knees low. We'll have red wing for dinner." He kissed the back of my head. "*Por nus-ya gohori*, Emyri."

Two deep, chest-rattling breaths as my black wing backed away from me, leaving me to face Dagon on my own. "*Por nus-ya gohori*," I said one last time. Power exploded like fire in my veins, burning behind my eyes and beneath my skin.

With reckless steps, I lunged forward, moving my body low as a Tru would if they were trying to hide in the underbrush. My muscles were accustomed to that motion—the way of hiding, sneaking, spying—and the red wing never saw it coming.

I hacked at his calf with all my strength, Nkita's sword in my hand colliding with Dag's bone so he hollered and fell sideways to the ground.

"Ow! You *knobsucker*!"

I raised my sword above my head, grabbing the hilt with two hands and ready to stop the red wing from hurting Nkita ever again.

"Enough," Nkita said, grabbing me by the back of the dress and tugging me away from Dagon. "Don't kill him. Not yet."

Dagon hissed and spewed, holding his leg. "That *bloodplucking* little—"

I lowered the sword, relief taking the place of the power that had wrecked my slender body. I was more than glad when Nkita took it from my hands.

"Now, if you don't mind," he said to me, "I might actually need some aid here. Things are starting to spin."

"But...but Dagon—"

"She *chopped* my *leg* off!" Dagon thundered. "That muckeating—"

"Your leg is fine," Nkita growled. "You deserve worse."

"Now it's my turn! *Again*."

"H-his...turn? Nkita...." I went to my mate and tiptoed, examining the narrow slit in his armor through which Dagon had sunk his sword. His aim had to be impeccable to accomplish it from above the way he did and his knowledge of Cryl armor unrivaled. I stored the information away for later and began unfastening that armor. I needed to get to Nkita's wound to apply pressure.

"This isn't a game we play, Dagon," Nkita said sternly. "How many times do I have to tell you—"

"I'll find you," Dagon said. "And I'll take my revenge. On the both of you." He smirked. "I like that there's a new little playmate. Maybe if you loosened up a bit, black wing, we could...share her—?"

I knew Nkita well enough to put my hand on his chest in preparation. His heartbeat slowed beneath my palm, which meant he was nigh to rage. "I will rip your head from your pathetic shoulders—"

"Nkita." I tried to pull his attention back to me.

Dagon sighed. "He's no fun, Goldie. No fun at all."

17

The Day The Vipers Writhed

Nkita sighed, frustrated. "Where's Miasi, soldier?"

When the General called him a soldier, Dag got serious and squirmed, unsettled for reasons I didn't understand. "Erm...I left her."

"Left her?" I asked.

"Hanging from a tree. North of here."

"You were *serious*?!" I cried.

Dag shrugged. "I don't owe you explanations. You chopped my leg off."

"Your leg is *fine*. Get up," I said. "Up, up."

Dagon frowned and hobbled to his feet. "Well... it *hurts*."

"You just tried to *kill* me!"

"I was only playing," he argued with a scowl. "What's *wrong* with her?" he asked Nkita.

"Me? Are you absolutely unhinged?"

Dagon shrugged, a bit saddened by my inquiry from the looks of his pout. Then, with no warning, he full-spread his wings and took off, plowing upward through the treetops. Gone.

"I hope we never see him again," I said, even though a small part of me found the red wing amusing. I ripped the hem of my skirt and pressed it to Nkita's shoulder. "What...just...happened?"

"No time," he replied. "The rebels should have caught us by now. Dagon has a habit of slowing me down. We must make haste."

"Nk—"

He took over the application of pressure to his wound, sheathed his sword, and left through the woods, headed north and expecting me to follow.

I hurried behind him, worried about the way he staggered every few steps. "You're hurt—"

"It's just blood."

"You need that, if I'm not mistaken. And a moment ago, you asked for my help."

"And you helped. I don't need blood, Em. I need you alive. I need you safe."

"*Nkita*—"

"I know when you're in danger, Emyri. It is the whole point of me now, isn't it? Perhaps it has always been the whole point of me. Quit arguing. We are out of time."

I stopped moving, digging my heels in and refusing to take another step. "Oh? Well, what is the whole point of me now? Why do you get to be the hero? Why do you get to be selfless—?"

"Woman—"

"*General! I will tie off your wound!*" I shouted. My fists trembled with anger at my sides. "I'm not losing you to a stupid red wing game."

He froze, his lilac eyes caught on my every move as I took another strip of fabric from my skirt, bunched the first bit on his wound, and then tied the second strip tightly around it. My fingers moved with ease, used to mending nets while I told my stories or polishing silver in the houses of the Teth in the Capital.

"There," I said. I touched his cheek, wishing I could climb into his lap and slow down with him. But no. He was right. We were in danger, and nothing would have been worse than the danger my heart and body would face if this Crylia were gone. "Let's find Miasi and then get you some water, General."

"She's this way," he said, sweat beading along his fine forehead. I'd seen Nkita struggle before. I'd seen him beaten, broken, his wing ripped from his shoulder. But I'd never seen him grow pale like this.

"What did he do to you? I don't understand?"

"He's more skilled than most Cryl think," Nkita explained.

"But...he's mad."

"So much skill will do that to a mind."

"I hope he's gone for good," I confessed out loud. "He needs to be gone."

"Oh no. He will be back. It's his turn."

"What are these *turns*?"

"She's up ahead." We came to a ridge that sloped down into a grassy area. "Your Queen. See her?"

There she was. And indeed she was up in a tree, dangling like a deer being bled for slaughter, the ropes pinning her arms to her side.

"Careful," Nkita said. "That blue-green grass. Wetgrass...."

I nodded, realizing what I'd almost stepped into. "Marsh."

"And from the sound of it, marsh vipers."

"You can hear them from here?"

He nodded. "Writhing and hissing, yes. Dagon must have tied the Queen there to make sure she didn't try to run. She would have surely met her end if she did."

"But Dagon...he had wings. He got her safely to the tree...."

"So I imagine."

"How...are we going to get her down, Nkita?"

He sighed, scrubbing at his perspiration with the back of his hand. "It's going to have to be you, Em."

My eyes widened. "Me?" How was I supposed to get across sopping-wet land and avoid marsh vipers, silk spiders, and whatever else lived beneath the grass? "Gua helps the helpless, Nkita, but—"

"Time to walk on water, Emyri Izela."

18

The Day The Rope Was Severed

I stared at my mate and when I was finished, I stared some more. Finally, I looked from him over to the tree where my Tru Queen was waiting to be rescued. Then I observed all the viper-infested marshland in between.

"Nkita...how—"

"I told you."

"I can't *do* that. Tru can't walk on water. Can...can *Crylia* do that?"

"We cannot."

"Then what in all of Miror are you thinking?"

He put his hand on my waist and pointed over the marsh. "Use your words. A Vessel is no Tonguekeeper as far as power and command, but you can access them just the same, Em. They can get you across."

Words, I knew well. I'd been a storyteller in my old Tru life, raised to understand the power words had to build community, to strengthen hope and resolve. Perhaps even to incite rebellions. But I did not possess any word knowledge that could help me rewrite Gua's laws and walk atop the surface of water. That, I could not do.

"*Nkita—*"

"Some make the mistake of thinking it's purely Old Cryl. But there's more to the Pure Tongue. The more? I don't know. But I can teach the Old Cryl bit. And with your power, Em, you can do these simple things."

"Simple?! I don't have *any* power. If I had power, do you think I'd have hidden as a spy in a hostile land? Or let Cyndr take me as a slave? Do you think I'd have let your wing be taken? I would have used it—"

"We have little time for your insecurity on this matter, Emyri. It's time to try."

I took a quick breath. He was right. No doubt he could already hear the rebels looking for us. Even if Rhaza defeated Hrogar, she would want the Pureblood Heir and his future Queen. It would be best for us to vacate this area, to find a way to get to Drosya. Nkita's Pure Blood they already craved, but they could not discover who *I* really was. They'd never let us go.

I ran my fingers over his knuckles as they squeezed my side. "Alright. What do I say?"

"*Sedayla-mekkim lyim.*"

"Slower. Please. Old Cryl sounds like someone gurgling water in their mouth."

"*Sedayla-mekkim lyim*," he said again, his deep voice surrounding me. And I swore when he spoke, the tiny pebbles and blades of wetgrass around us began to react.

"You can do it without me?" I asked, studying the stones that began to hover.

"Not even close," he answered. "Now try."

"*Sedayla-mekkim lyim*," I said, stumbling through the words.

"Get your mind to agree with your speech, please, Emyri. We haven't got all day."

I squirmed. "You could be more *polite*—"

"You could be more *efficient*."

"Must we argue every moment—?"

"Em, *say the damn words!*"

I took an angry breath. "*Sedayla-mekkim lyim!*"

Then, my partner placed his hands on my lower back and shoved me forward. With a squeal, I stumbled, my arms flailing as I prepared to sink into the marsh. But I found my feet coasting over the wetgrass, the water making squelching noises beneath my shoes.

"Nkita, are you insane?!" I huffed, realizing in a panic that he'd just endangered my life on a belief, albeit not misled, that I could do these sorts of undoable things.

"You're the one who insists on risking our lives to save this Queen. Now get her."

I grumbled about how arrogant and willful my black wing was and how he was convinced he knew everything and that he was always right when, in fact, sometimes I was right and it was perfectly acceptable for me to be wary of stepping out onto the marsh when no one had bothered to tell me exactly what being the last Vessel entailed or what the Tonguekeeper was actually supposed to do.

Beneath my feet, through the murky waters of the marsh, I saw twisting, spiraling white vipers, their scales poking through the garish surface and bumping against my boots.

"Nkita...."

"Speed will aid you in evasion."

"You tell me that *now*?"

"Oh, because you have been the most apt listener—?"

I ignored him, hastening my steps until I reached the tree and climbed up. My body felt worn, almost as if I'd run for miles and miles. Perhaps speaking the Old Cryl did take power from me after all. But, I was able to hoist myself all the way to where Miasi hung.

"I should have brought a knife," I panted.

"*Reizat-te*," Nkita called out over the water, no doubt realizing my conundrum as I tried to untangle Dagon's knots with my fingers while Miasi's body twirled like a hare in a trap.

"Not again," I mumbled. "More Old Cryl?"

"Izela?"

I looked up at Miasi when her voice floated over me. "You're not hurt, are you?"

"Only my pride. And it will recover."

"Good. When I see that red wing next, I'll—"

"Thank you." She interrupted me. "For coming to get me."

When I looked up at Miasi, there were tears in her eyes.

I nearly growled at her. "Stop that. I will deal with whatever this display of nonsensical emotion is later, Mia. For now, let me figure out this Old Cryl and get you down." *Of course I've come for her. I'll always come for her, no matter the cost.* I licked my lips, but for the life of me, I could not remember what nonsense words Nkita had said. "One more time?" I shouted.

"The rebels are closing in, Emyri!"

"Then *tell me the words*, General! Cryl be damned!"

"*Tru* be damned!"

"*Nkita!*"

"*Reizat-te!*"

"Alright!"

"*Say* it!"

"...*Reizat-te.*" The ropes split into a thousand pieces without warning, and I grabbed hold of Miasi just in time for her weight to send us both toppling out of the tree and careening toward the vipers. The water met my skin in a blast of sticky warmth and sucked me down into its depths in an instant. I gagged as the thickness flooded my mouth and nose. I thought only of getting Miasi to safety. Until...fangs like daggers sank themselves into my flesh, the viper they belonged to locking its wide open jaw to my breast and refusing to unhinge.

After that, I did not think so much of Miasi or her safety. Or of Nkita and how terribly sad he might be that I died so young. I thought not of Drosya being taken to the Cza or Dagon and his meddling ways. Not of the rebels and their demands to make Nkita royalty.

No.

I thought only of the venom throbbing in my veins and how truly tired I'd become as my entire being went cold...and then perfectly numb.

19

The Day the General Knelt

I was becoming far too familiar with the rough grip of Cyndr's meaty hands on my person. It was short-lived though, for Nkita growled at him and he let me go, my body laid out on the dry dirt. Numbness faded to a slow, throbbing pain, and I had the urge to sit up.

"Easy," Nkita said, his hand on my back as he helped me. "Em, I need to get the venom out." My vision was hazy, but I could make out the black wing motioning to Cyndr. "Hold her arms down."

He took his blade out and slid it across the upper area of my right breast, then squeezed. When I didn't fight him or squirm, he paused, groping my face and getting me to look right at him. I knew him well enough to tell he was worried. Still crouching, he put his mouth on me and sucked at the incision, pulling as much venom out of me as he could.

A sharp, piercing pain ran through my skull, and I groaned, heat rushing through my veins. "Miasi," I finally said. "Where is she?"

"You first," Nkita replied.

Something in his tone told me not to question him.

He turned me, running his blade through my left forearm and repeating his action, drawing out the poison. I hadn't realized I'd been bitten more than once. Again, he took care of the flesh on my outer thigh. Then he worked his hands over me, checking for more bites.

"Miasi...?"

"She's alright."

I put a shaking hand on his chest, hoping to slow him down. His lilac eyes shimmered with intensity. He was more than concerned. Nkita was afraid.

"I'm alright."

"You are now...."

"I don't want to die. I don't want Miasi to die."

"I—"

"I have given up too much to protect her. It wouldn't be fair. It wouldn't be fair if she died now. She has to live."

"Em...."

"You've given up too much to protect me. It wouldn't be fair to you if I died, would it?" I shook my head, trying to slow down my thoughts, but they rushed out of my lips with increasing speed. "I've never liked Tru food. I prefer the flavors of the Capital. But I can't tell anyone, or they'll think I've become a traitor. Yet, it's the truth.

And I always thought Mahopi was quite handsome. Nearly as handsome as you. Maybe sometimes more handsome. He has such dynamic features, and you're both so pretty when you're cross. He's isn't the best kisser. It should not have factored into my decision to leave him as much as it did, but sometimes little things matter. Like when you make that little sound when you"—my vision cleared, objects becoming extremely detailed and the air growing cold as it raced through my nose and mouth.

"What's wrong with her?" Cyndr asked. "Why is she saying all these things?"

"The venom," Nkita explained. "It's bringing truth to her lips. We're fortunate that's how her blood reacts with it." He reached down and ripped a piece of my dress's hem, using it to gag my mouth. "This could be far worse."

"I want to know what she says," Cyndr argued as he stood to full height. "We could learn things—"

Nkita rose up, going chest to chest with the enormous slaver. "And that is exactly why *I* am her mate, and not someone like you." He crouched beside me once more, putting his hand on my cheek. He never held emotion in his features. Not the way Tru did. But he felt deeply. The more I understood this, the more I could see it in his eyes, feel it in the shocks his fingertips sent through me. "I'll see to your friend now. You'll be alright."

I didn't have to worry about Cyndr with Nkita present. But, I realized that if the slaver was with us, it meant the rebels had caught us after all. And it also meant Rhaza had taken control from Hrogar.

"He favors you too much," Cyndr whispered so only I could hear. "It's going to get him killed."

Oh, I know. I know I'm his greatest weakness. But what can I do? There's nowhere I can go where he won't come for me. There's no one I can pretend to be that he won't love.

"We need him," Cyndr said. "We will never be free without him. We will never be anything without him."

That's exactly how I feel.

Rhaza parted the brush and came toward us, her sword still tight in her hand and the blood of Cryl splattered against her skin and clothes. She was different than any Cryl female I'd ever beheld.

"It's taken care of," she said with a nod. "The Queen lives?"

"Yes," Cyndr said. "But the Pureblood Heir does not wish to remain with us, Rhaza."

She turned sharp eyes to where Nkita must have been working on Miasi. "We need you."

Nkita returned, wiping blood from his chin with his sleeve. "There is much you don't understand. My situation is complicated."

"The Cza must be stopped, and the only way we can divert power from his line is through you. Tethers will be broken. Your tether would be broken. You could form new ones. The Teth will have choices once more: to join him or to join you. An army can be formed. A proper army. One that chooses to fight for Crylia. Not forced. Not threatened. We only ask that you take your rightful place and give us a chance to side with you. A chance to be free."

"I hear your plight, Rhaza...."

She balled her fist at her side. "But you refuse to help?"

"I have a greater destiny than the one you see for me."

"There is nothing more important than what I am asking of you."

"I can say no more—"

"Then how am I supposed to simply let you walk away from us? From the Cryl I have gathered who are ready to fight for you with their very lives? At risk of losing everything?"

"You tell them that if they see me as their Cza, they will allow me to do what I must."

Rhaza sighed. "They...will lose hope. If you leave us so soon, I"—she cleared her throat—"I will lose hope."

"I did not ask for this rebellion."

"I did not ask for this Cza. For this war against the humans. Against...so many races and kinds. I have never asked for anything I've been dealt. But I am asking now...for you."

"I have a proposal."

All fell silent when Miasi spoke. She limped forward, reaching out for Cyndr to take her arm. The Cryl offered his support, no doubt without realizing he was yielding to her. Such was the might of the Tru Queen. She never demanded. She only moved in quiet power. And she wore that look on her face—the one that meant she was decreeing something of utmost importance, that everyone should listen since she did not intend to raise her voice.

Her dress was tattered and drenched, blood from where Nkita cut her staining the white. Dark circles ringed her usually serene eyes.

"You?" Rhaza asked.

"I, Miasi, Queen of the Tru, have a proposal."

"Go on, Tru Queen," Nkita said, his deep voice warning the others to listen.

Miasi raised her chin. "I will remain here with the rebels and will rally whatever Tru forces remain. I will also do all I can to reach any other human tribes in Miror to aid the rebel cause. This will be the first known alliance between Tru and Crylia."

Rhaza's eyes widened. "You...I...."

"I have two conditions."

"Speak them," Rhaza said.

"First, we must declare the rebels a separate faction, completely removed from the rulership of the Cza of Crylia, as we will never ally with such a being as him. Second, I will only accept rulership of the new faction from Nkita Opas, though it may take him time to assume this position. I am willing to grant him that time, for he is correct in the belief that his current task is more important than anything. Which brings me to my third point." She looked at Rhaza. "I want you declared Queen Regent of this new faction."

Rhaza barked out a laugh. "Me?! No Crylia male will ever call me their sole leader."

"If they want their freedom, the cost will be their pride." Miasi did not falter, nor did she hesitate or stutter. "I will not bring my people into your ranks, otherwise. If they cannot accept you, how will they ever accept us?"

Nkita nodded. "Miasi's wisdom is evident. This is the only way I will agree to become your Cza. You want your hope, Rhaza, then this is how you secure it."

To my surprise, Rhaza looked to Cyndr. "Would you?" she asked, her voice more timid than usual. "Would you ever consider me your Queen and commander?"

Cyndr huffed. "No."

Rhaza nodded. "I...."

"But if it means the Pureblood will take his place on his throne, I will pretend to."

Nkita nodded. "Very well. That will have to be enough."

"Great Cza..." Rhaza began.

"Hopefully you are a strong enough white wing to carry all three of us back to the camp," Nkita said. He knelt in the dirt. "I am in need of rest."

With that, my heart rattled in my chest. My black wing had never acted so strangely, not even after the vicious battles he fought for the Cza. *What has Dagon done to him?*

20

The Day The Truth Was Spilled

Miasi insisted on being placed with me in one of the better tents of the rebel campground. As soon as we were left alone, she uncovered my mouth and wrapped her arms around me.

"Oh Izela, you scared me. I thought I'd lost you."

"Yet you didn't seem too worried about my well-being when you let the council send me out to spy or to perish. I don't remember you having any messengers deliver letters. I don't remember you caring at all. In fact, you were rather preoccupied with your Queenly duties. Even now, you are making political moves rather than caring. Rather than truly caring. You would have had me marry—"

I clamped my own hand over my mouth, my eyes filling with tears. I couldn't stop myself from saying exactly the truth, no matter how it hurt. And oh, it hurt.

Miasi swallowed. "I'm...sorry...."

I shook my head, my hand still over my mouth.

"It's alright," she said, removing my hand. "You can say whatever you want, Izzy."

"I did it for you," I blurted out. Hot tears slipped down my cheeks. "And you didn't even care."

"Of course I cared. I care still. An immense amount." She smoothed my hair back even though we both looked absolutely horrendous. "I don't know what else to say."

"You wish I hadn't done it. What I did."

To my surprise, she stifled a sob, her serene composure cracking. "I only wish it didn't hurt you like it did. It's my fault—"

"It was *his* fault, and we both know it." I inhaled shaky breaths. "And I'm *glad* your father's dead. I'd kill him again. If Gua took me back in time, I'd choose the same." I put my hand on her cheek. "But I wish you'd taken better care of me. Yet, I am also glad you didn't because now, I met this black wing. And I think he's worth it, Mia. I think...he might be worth the whole thing."

"Then...." She struggled through her tears. "I'll make sure you get to keep him. I owe you both *so much*. I will repay it, Izzy."

"I don't like when you call me Izela. Not anymore." More truths. So many. A spy is entitled to keep those. "It was my name before, but when I left the tribe, I had to change everything about myself. It was more than having my back scarred to look like I once had wings. It was more than piercing my lip to put a Grounded ring in it. I had to become someone *new*. I had to become

Em in my mind. So that Em could become Syiva. And Oahra. And now, she's been pretending to be Izzy for you again, and I just cannot *pretend* anymore. You mean too much to me. If I'm going to be anyone to you, I want you to understand that Izela died when she left Tru."

Miasi bit her lip and then gave a curt nod. "*Emyri.*" She sniffled, trying to be strong. "The water suits you, Emyri of the Tru."

My heart swelled with relief. To be understood...it was a blessing I didn't think I was worthy of. "The rivers are yours, Queen Miasi." I paused. "Wait. Why aren't you speaking the truth? Weren't you bitten?"

"The black wing said the vipers chose something else for me when the venom mixed with my blood."

"What...Miasi, what did they choose?"

"Pain." She gave a feeble smile. "But it is wearing off. Have no fear. And your blight too seems to be waning."

"I should not have burdened you with all this when you were in so much pain...." My stomach clenched with the realization that I'd been a worse friend than I realized.

"I am skilled at bearing it," she assured me.

"You spoke like a Tru Queen even while you were hurting, Mia. I was so proud."

"Really? You think it was a good idea? My proposal?"

"It buys us time and buys you and whomever remains of our people some semblance of protection. Nkita and I...we need to find the Tonguekeeper."

"Of course."

"*Nkita!*" I gasped, stumbling off the cot and away from Miasi. "He had better be alright. I swear, if that black wing died on me, I'll kill him."

The moment I opened the flap of the tent, the black wing snatched me, his arm around my waist.

"Off to cause me trouble?"

I pressed against him without hesitation, breathing in the scent of his freshly bathed body. "I thought *you* were misbehaving. I thought I was going to have to hunt your soul down and drag it back to your body."

"I am right here, Em. You worry too much."

I couldn't say anything else. All my wit and banter stilled on my tongue.

"This way," Nkita said, lifting me and walking me back the way he must have come from. "Let me look at you."

In the lone tent, he sat me on his cot, then lit the oil lamp that hung from one of the poles. Then, he came over to me, close enough for me to squirm with desire.

"You're still in pain," I whispered. I ran my hand over his shoulder, glad to see him without his armor for the first time in a long time. "What did Dagon do? I don't understand."

Nkita took my fingers and directed them to the place where Dagon had inserted his dagger. "There. We Crylia have blood vessels that run here, over our shoulders. They supply our wings. It's a known tactic to aim for those to bleed out an enemy. But it takes incredible skill to perforate armor in exactly the right place."

"Dagon...wanted to kill you?"

"He was showing off, is all. I have no wing on this side. If I did, it would have pulsed out more blood and it would have been the end of me. He knew it wouldn't kill me. But weaken me? Yes"

"I want this game between you to come to an end."

"He's harmless," Nkita assured me. "Except for when he is very, very dangerous. But enough talk of the red wing." He ran his calloused fingers over my temples, my jaw. "Let me see to you."

"You've seen to me enough."

"I should not have let you cross the wetgrass."

"You didn't know I would be so clumsy."

To my awe, he kissed me, his lips a cold surprise. "You were valiant," he said, pausing to examine the snake bites on my body.

"You had to *push me* out onto the swamp."

"You refused to leave your friend."

"My Queen? I had to—"

"You didn't go to her because you're patriotic, Em. You went to Miasi because you're loyal. And kind beyond measure. It's why you always run from me. And it's why you stay as well."

"Oh?" My voice cracked with emotion as he kissed my neck. "Now you think you know me so well?"

"I might need to refresh my memory."

I gasped as his mouth reached my breasts, his soft kisses growing in intensity as he soothed my wounds. "I thought you'd be too weakened. Too...*tired*—"

He growled. "How do you always know what will make me angry? What special talent is this?"

"It's called being a woman. Now...maybe a little rest for my black wing?" I teased.

"I'll sleep all I want," he said, his lilac eyes holding mine steady, the challenge in them clear, "after I make you pay for refusing to do what you're told."

I swallowed, my throat suddenly dry. "Refusing? I'm afraid I don't know what you mean...." I knew very well what he meant. My heartbeat filled my ears, my breath catching in my throat.

"You have no idea what being Teth-wed is supposed to be like, do you, Em?"

"Mm.... 'Lie very still' is the extent of my knowledge. And that it's supposed to hurt. Sometimes. If we're apart."

"I don't require the first. And the second, I don't expect. But—"

"You don't?"

He grabbed me and turned so that I sat on his lap, straddling him. Then, he lighted a kiss on my lips.

"You're not like Cryl. Not like...me. It doesn't hurt you to be apart. I have come to accept this."

"Oh." *I should tell him. I should tell him that missing him almost drove me mad. That the pain in my body was undeniable. That the longing in my soul almost crippled me.* But for reasons I could not identify, I said none of this and I let him think I was invincible and unaffected. I lied. By my silence. I lied to him.

"But what I will not accept," Nkita said, lifting my dress with one hand, his fingers digging into my thighs as he slid them up my leg, "is your bold disobedience."

"You want me to blindly obey your commands? To go when you say 'go'? To come when you say 'come'?" I laughed against his lips. "You'll never have that from me, General."

"Then what was the point of falling in love with you, hm?"

I bit his lip. "You like your prey to put up a little fight, is all. Tell me I'm wrong...."

"My prey?"

I leaned even closer to him, not minding the shot of pain through my injured breast as it pressed against his chest. I whispered in his ear. "Soon, General, perhaps I'll be the predator, and you'll be at my mercy, following my orders. I'll be carrying you to safety. Seems like that's what's in store for the two of us...don't you agree?"

The look in his sharp eyes changed as they narrowed. He put that strong hand around my neck. But this time he didn't wait for me to return the gesture before throwing me back onto the blankets.

21

THE DAY THE CRIMSON FELL

My mind couldn't decide whether I should be excited or afraid.

The black wing gripped my hip with one hand and yanked me downward, thrusting himself into me so sharply that my only response was to lose my voice, my back arching as I held tight to the worn blankets on his cot.

I'd never seen Nkita change forms while he was with me. It had always been saved for adversaries, for...battle. But now his irises narrowed, his talons stretching from his fingertips and tearing lines of pain down the surface of my skin. Striations of black fur rose on his neck, disappearing beneath the collar of his shirt, his wing full-spread as if he wished to take flight.

I shuddered at the realization that he could become what I'd seen Rizel become. That he could turn into a beast much more formidable than any I'd seen. A true, terrifying monster. *And what lies beyond that? How far can a Crylia take its monstrous form?*

I searched for my voice. Not to tell the black wing to stop, but to ground myself. To assure myself that I had some semblance of strength to bring to the exchange. But Nkita's hand around my neck tightened, and all my body could manage was trembling as pleasure coursed through me.

Pricks of black and white cluttered my vision, and my being began to relax, my muscles loosening their grip, control and compulsion waning as I chose to let go.

Finally, heat took its place, and my heart rate began to soar once more, so loud and fast that my fear battled with desire once more. But, desire had its way and my muscles went taut, my body convulsing before, at last, relaxing beneath my mate.

But he was not finished with me.

Before he could think, he turned me over, my belly on the cot as he lifted my dress shoving it up my waist with a growl. His palm on the back of my head, he used his free hand to lift my hips, entering me once more without hesitation.

"Admit it," he said, his voice crawling over my skin. "Tell me I was your choice."

I groaned into the blankets, my breath ragged as every sensation clawed at me all at once. It took only a few more thrusts for my groan to become a whimper. But I would not confess.

Am I truly this stubborn? It's the truth. I could say it. I could tell him how I feel, what is really going on in both my mind and my heart.

But he finished before I dared be vulnerable. He finished before I could reveal my heart. He finished in as much anger as he had started and rose, his deep voice rumbling as he spoke. "You must think I'm one of your human suitors," he said. "You must think I'm a fool. You must think I'm...kind." He leaned over me, sank his talons into my hair, and gripped, lifting my head so his lips could touch my ears. "But you are *my mate*. And that means I will *break* you, Emyri Izela. I do not take my time with you because I'm *noble*. Don't be mistaken. I take my time with you because you're *mine*."

He released me and stood up, and I turned in time to see him fastening his trousers.

"You won't get me to believe you're not noble," I managed, my voice hoarse. "I know you."

"Your wounds are bleeding," he replied, his voice monotone. "You delude yourself into thinking I've never done anything wrong. You test me as if I'm to be as perfect as your Gua. I am warning you. I am far from it."

"Nkita—"

"The *only* reason—and mind you, it is the *only* one—that I have not slaughtered everyone you've ever loved, including your precious Queen—is because I am bonded to you as my mate."

I licked dry lips, a wave of panic washing over me. "You...wouldn't hurt—"

"I did. For years. And I would have continued for all my days. If not for the Cza, then I would have done it for myself, in my own name. You all urge me to take up the crown of Crylia but you have not considered who you're actually mated to. You have not considered what sort of Cza I would be. I am *Crylia*, Emyri. An opportunist? Yes. A rebel? Perhaps. A fool for falling in love with you? Most certainly. But I am not always patient. And I am not always good. I urge you to *mind my anger*." He nudged a metal basin with the toe of his boot. "I'll draw you a bath. You'll need your rest if we are to take the life of the Tonguekeeper and transfer her power to you."

And with that, the mate I was certain I knew left me sitting in a pool of his mess, my head throbbing, my hands shaking, and the wounds from the fangs of vipers leaking crimson down the length of my golden skin.

22

THE DAY THE  WATER STIRRED

I sat in the bath alone, brooding, running my fingers through the warm water Nkita had prepared for me and wondering what Gua would have to say about all this if she had to walk around on two legs like I did. I was thankful, though, that she did not live a life like mine. She wouldn't be Gua. Who would I have to depend on then?

I'd known, in the back of my mind, that Nkita Opas was not easy or simple or easily changed. And I knew that the bond between us could not make him truly love my people. He wouldn't harm them. But he wouldn't love them either.

We were different. No matter how I felt about him or how he felt about me...we were Tru and Crylia. Enemies, our hearts stitched together with little more than defiance, lust, and fate. It would never truly work. We would force it to for as long as possible. We would cling to what we wanted the other person to provide for us. For me, it was a place to come home to and someone who did not care what I'd done. For him, he wanted someone who made his life interesting and rich, who did not lie still like all the other female Cryl.

What do I do, Gua? Who do I pretend to be now?

"Do I call you Queen *Syiva* or Queen *Emyri*? Cyndr says you were once called *Oahra*...."

My gaze settled on Rhaza as she entered Nkita's tent. "Are you here for the General? He went off to hunt, he said."

"I'm here for no reason at all." She sighed, squatting before the basin where I bathed. I would have longed for some privacy if I felt I was entitled to any. Rhaza had saved my life. *Why shouldn't she be able to look at me?* "At least that's what it feels like these days."

"Pointless? All of it?"

"For me? Yes. For Crylia, maybe I can make a difference before I die. Who knows?" She motioned to me, beckoning me to give her my hand. "A Queen should not bathe herself."

I kept my arms at my sides. "I have been no one important my entire life. I cannot be expected to change that so quickly."

Rhaza chuckled. "Humor me. I like to imagine you are truly our Sovereign and I have succeeded." She gestured again. "Let us pretend."

I sighed, giving her my hand and letting her pool water onto my skin. "Rhaza? Why did you save us from the Cza? Just so Nkita could rule?"

"Mm. Yes."

"Why not save only him? Leave me behind?"

"He would not have gone without you."

"Because he loves me."

"Because you are mates, and that's not how Crylia do things." She locked knowing gray eyes on me. "You know...I could help you, my Queen. You can only learn so much from the ways of *male* Cryl. And we must make the rebels believe you are one of us. It's bad enough that you're playing the part of a Grounded. That I actually am Grounded. We must be convincing. More convincing than any male has ever had to be."

"I've seen Crylia mates hate each other. Despise each other. Ruin each other."

"You think...he does love you?"

"I think he does."

"Well, that's unfortunate for him."

I grinned. "That's what I've been saying."

"You're clever. You see what others can't."

My smile faded. There was so much I could not see. So many secrets being kept from me. "Rhaza?"

"Yes...?"

"Call me Em. And...would you tell me more? About the Pureblood Heir. I should have a better understanding if I am to play my part in all this. And Nkita speaks like...like...."

"Like a black wing." Rhaza nodded with a smirk. "What do you already know? I will do my best to inform you. I am more knowledgeable than most regarding this matter."

Good. This is good. "I know Nkita is of some ancient Cryl bloodline that gives him the right to be Cza, the right to form tethers with nobles. I know that the Cza knew this and did not destroy Nkita, a fact I do not understand."

"Why would the Cza allow a rival to live, you wonder?"

"Exactly. It's not kindness that compels the Cryl...."

"No. No, it is most certainly not. But the King was sure to keep Nkita's nest close. To make sure he was tethered to him at birth. The Pureblood Heir as a Teth makes the Cza ten times more powerful."

"So he takes the risk of a mutiny...for the sake of power?"

"Nkita will *not* kill the Cza while he serves him as a Teth. He *can* but he will not. It would ruin him."

"Then...how can Nkita become Cza while another Cza is ruling?"

"He must stake his claim to Crylia and he must be declared viable by the Mirorian Zenith so all tethers are broken."

"The...*who*?"

Rhaza hesitated, biting her ringed lip. "Not many Cryl will know of this. Not unless they are of the elites in the Capital. Your ignorance will go undetected for most. But...."

"Please tell me, Rhaza." *Information is always more valuable than gold.* "It can do no harm for me to know. I assure you."

She nodded. "The Zenith is an ancient order. And Miror is bound to it, even if its rulers like to believe they are not. The Tonguekeeper presides over the four: the Crylia, the humans, the Bahari, and the Ven. All five together choose the fate of the world."

I scoffed. "Those are stories, Rhaza. No such things as Bahari and Ven exist. We'd be drowned in monsters if that were the case. The Crylia are enough." I cleared my throat, realizing my blunder. "Not that every Cryl is a monster—"

"I understand your confusion. This is what most of us are taught to believe. But the Bahari and the Ven exist as surely as the humans and Crylia do, and their rulers are part of the Zenith. Without their consent, a new bloodline cannot rise to rule any one of the crowns."

"So...the Cza rules the Crylia. And the humans are ruled by...Miasi? But there are other human tribes which are not Tru—"

"It is who the Zenith chose to represent the humans. The line of Queen Miasi of the Tru."

"But...we Tru are not *mighty*."

"You were chosen all the same. And Miasi is a Pureblood Heir of your people."

I shook my head. "Why is the Cza fighting the Tru? Why fight one of the Zenith?"

"To eliminate your people. To remove you from the Zenith."

It all made sense. "Remove Miasi, and another Tru will be chosen. But remove *all* the Tru.... That must mean...something happened. Between Tru and Crylia. Long ago. The Czas must have had a reason for believing the Tru wish to pass the Cryl crown to another."

"So we are led to believe, yes."

"With the Tru gone, another human tribe would be chosen, unaware of the histories and endgames of the previous rulers. They couldn't hope to match the power he gains."

"A very possible outcome."

"This...this whole war...is not between Crylia and Tru. It is between the Cza and the Zenith. They are not dealing in blood or land or customs, they are dealing in crowns and destinies."

"You understand."

"You are being smart, Rhaza. Forcing the Zenith to choose a new Crylia heir to wear the crown is *brilliant*. It saves the Tru from this merciless war. If Miasi is willing to elect Nkita—" *And if the* Tonguekeeper *is willing. That is why Nkita wants to find Drosya. Not because she is a kind old Cryl who needs protection, but because she can cast her vote for Nkita. And if she won't....*

They'll have her choose me so that I will choose them.

"Rhaza, but what about the other monsters? The Bahari and the Ven? I cannot believe they truly roam this world. I've never seen one. I've never even heard of anyone who has."

"We will face their horrors when it's time. When we must." She narrowed her eyes, her bird-like nose twitching. "They will say yes to our new Cza. To our Pureblood Heir. They won't have a choice."

Will I? I swallowed, watching as Rhaza poured water over my naked body. *Cryl be damned, little spy. You are nothing more than a pawn in the hands of ruthless players. Time to start paying attention.*

23

The Day The Spy Prepared

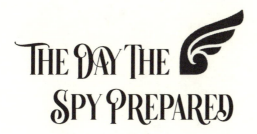

Don't let him know you know.

I did my very best not to appear as skittish as I felt when Nkita walked past me on his way to some strategist meeting with Cyndr. I was sure Hrogar should have been in attendance, but I hadn't heard a word about the one-eyed gray wing since our return to the rebel camp.

Instead of wondering what had come of him, I put my attention toward the rather lengthy lecture Rhaza was giving me. In her breeches and mud-stained shirt, she looked nothing like the high class Teth-wed Cryl female she was pretending to be.

"Chin high," she explained, demonstrating by tilting her head back. "And when you walk you must both flounce and glide. Like there's wind under your feet with each step. Like so." She bopped and floated around the tent. "Arms must be held out, so they never touch your sides."

I wrinkled my nose. "But...why? Don't their arms grow tired?"

"Oh, very tired, yes. But the posture is to make it easy for your male to put his arm around and take you away at any moment."

I scoffed. "Take me away?"

"Yes. If he has sudden needs, for example, or if some Crylia is speaking to you who ought not to be."

I exhaled, already frustrated. "Surely you are joking, Rhaza."

"I am being very serious. Now, let me see those arms out."

I lifted my arms so they curved slightly, hovering away from my body, and tried to bop and walk about. "Nkita did not explain all this when he prepared me for the Vecherins back in the Capital."

"The males do not know why we females do what we do. Most of them only know someone is doing poorly when they see it done poorly." She corrected the position of my arms, arching and posing each of my fingers so they were taut and separate from one another. "Stiffer movements. Quicker. More defined." Rhaza waved her hand through the air in a fluid motion. "You move like water. It's too Tru. You need to move as Crylia do. Less like the river, more like a bird." She nodded. "Now, look to the right and let me see."

I glanced to the right, my head twitching but the movement smooth. "Better?"

"Much better. It will make you sore at first, but you'll grow accustomed. And remember, Teth-wed are not aggressive. No fighting, no sharp words. Submit. Succumb. If you need help, you only hope it comes. Do not cry out. Do not scream. Do not argue. Do not run. Your survival relies exclusively on the strength and attentiveness of your Teth mate."

I lowered my arms. "Similar to being a Crylia servant, then? At least in that regard."

She nodded. "But with prettier gowns." Rhaza folded in her lips. "I admire your resilience. For me, I vowed never to return to the Capital. I've…had enough."

"You shouldn't have to go back, Rhaza." I looked around at the makeshift tent and the gathering of rebels who moved about, making plans for battles and futures, all of which relied on my ability to lie with great accuracy. "I will do my best to ensure your tomorrow looks nothing like your yesterday."

"I have faith that you will. I saw how you waited for our Pureblood Heir when he was being punished by the Feigning Cza. Your endurance is as strong as Nkita's."

"Feigning Cza?"

"I am tired of calling him what he's not. Nkita Opas will be Cza to me from now on." She cleared her throat. "Gives me hope to think of it that way."

Gives me fear. But she doesn't need to know that. And fear is an important part of being a Crylia female. I'll need it. "Do you think I'm ready to go? We shouldn't waste time, Rhaza."

"It would take you a lifetime to learn all the ways, my Queen. But remember this, and the rest will be well enough. In the Capital, you are not Nkita's partner. You are not friends. You are not a match. You belong to your mate. You are his to command, to use, to disregard. If you can fit yourself into that role, you will not find yourself in too much trouble."

I sighed. "Yielding is not my strongest suit. But...this is important. I will pretend."

"You may have to convince yourself it is so, Emyri."

"Syiva," I corrected her. "The Grounded, gold-wing Teth-wed to First General Opas. And only Nkita may call me Em."

Rhaza nodded, understanding that I needed to prepare myself for the elaborate ruse I was about to play. "I hardly recognize you," she said.

"Good," I replied. "I've already forgotten who I was."

Goodbye Emyri of the Tru-ori.

Hello Syiva of the Crylia monsters.

24

The Day the Story Was Silenced

"You'll meet with our rebel spy, Grigor, in Yogdn," Rhaza said as we walked away from the camp. "He will help get you safely to the castle of the Feigning Cza and he will have the names of the rebels within the castle who you can trust." She paused, studying the trees, perhaps lost in thought for a moment. "May I know your plans, my Cza? I...don't doubt you. But, I am concerned."

"I will do what must be done to make sure Em is safe."

Rhaza looked at me, then back to Nkita. "And you? Who will keep you safe? Your mate is lovely, but she cannot take the place of the Feigning Cza. We need you."

"If I die, there will be no one to protect my mate. And so, I will not die." He stared at the Queen Regent with those piercing lilac eyes as if things truly were so simple.

"We can't go until I say goodbye to Miasi," I said, scanning the campground in the distance, waiting. Finally, I saw her hurrying up the hill toward us, her dress gathered in her hands. Once she made it to me, she threw her arms around me.

"Em. My dearest friend. Please be safe."

I hugged her back. "I will."

"Lie very well."

I chuckled. "I always do."

"And don't forget who you are."

I hesitated. But then I nodded. "I won't." I kissed her forehead. "Please be safe. And may Gua guide you as you find the surviving Tru to join the rebels. May Gua guide you in all you do." I choked back my worry. "You'll...pray for me, won't you, Queen Miasi of the Tru?"

"I pray for you more often than anyone else," she confessed. "Nothing will ever change that. Even when I'm buried, I will pray for you, Emyri Izela. Even then."

I turned to leave, hurrying into the trees as words bubbled up from my heart, spilling out of my mouth. It had been so long. So long since a story demanded to escape me without my permission. But this one was coming whether I liked it or not.

"I...need to find water," I mumbled, hoping Nkita heard me.

"We will find some eventually," he replied. "On the way to the Capital—"

"I need to find water...now."

"We—"

I left him, setting a pace and angling myself for where I knew water flowed. I didn't need much. Only enough for me to soak the soles of my feet.

"Em, what are you doing? We've just set out. Do I need to throw you over my shoulder already?"

"I need water. For a moment."

We came upon the tiniest of brooks, and I stepped into the trickle. I exhaled, my shoulders relaxing. I always tried to forget these truths about me. That I wasn't ever supposed to be a spy. That I wasn't supposed to be Teth-wed or Grounded or anything else but what I was born to be. A storyteller.

With my next exhale came the words I'd been holding back.

"The night I ended my own life, the moon was only half over Miror. The air was warmer than it ever had been in Crylia but it held a familiar bite, as if the land knew things were about to change, as if Gua had fallen asleep and left me all alone. No one helped me that night. It was I who had done all the helping. It was I who would pay for it. Now, I will tell you the story of the Tru girl who did the right thing."

Nkita lifted me, moving me out of the brook and setting me on dry land. "What are you doing?" he asked, breathless, his brow furrowed in concern.

I shrugged. "Telling a story." I could not find the right words to explain to a Crylia what urge had taken over me. How could he ever understand? Cryl seemed to do whatever they wanted whenever they wanted it.

He tucked my hair behind my ear. "The venom still flows through you?"

"No." I shook my head, still in a daze. "It's not venom. It's a story." *It's my story.* The one I usually held back for myself. That one I kept hidden deep inside me. *Why is it coming out now? There are so many other stories I could tell. So many other stories that wouldn't hurt me to speak aloud.*

"Then tell me a different one, storyteller."

"Gua...wants *this* one."

"Good thing she isn't real."

"Nkita!" His words stung me, though I knew he spoke out of ignorance.

"Come on," he said, gripping my wrist and tugging me forward. "If she's real, she's no friend of yours."

"I'm a storyteller. I'm supposed to be telling stories."

"But you don't *want* to tell that one. If this Gua is forcing you to do something that brings you pain, she's my enemy. As undesired as viper venom flooding your veins."

"Do not make *enemies* with my goddess."

"Don't tell stories that rip my heart out," he growled.

I gasped, tears pricking my eyes. "You...you felt that?"

"I feel *everything* that hurts you, Emyri Izela. How many times must I explain it? Are you stubborn or stupid?"

A bit of both. I struggled against the warmth and comfort that flooded me as my mate held my wrist and led me forward, against the hope that gripped my bones when I let myself believe he really did love me, because I'd need to be more than a storyteller, more than a mate, more than a spy when we got to the Capital. In order to save Drosya from the Feigning Cza, from the Pureblood Heir, and from myself, I'd need to be *ruthless*.

25

The Day The General Lost His Mind

Two hours into our journey, and my bones began to chatter, the cold biting my skin and burning my fingertips and palms. I thought, in at least some small ways, I might have missed it. The shameless cold and the gray skies, the piercing thorns of the underbrush and the rugged, rocky paths slick with ice. The Crylia woodlands were familiar, but they were not at all missed.

"You're quiet," Nkita said in his deep way, his voice threatening to pull me closer to him.

"I suppose I am."

"Why? It's not like you."

"I can be quiet sometimes," I replied.

"Are you too cold?"

"I'm alright, Nkita. Really. Just…preparing my mind to re-enter Yogdn. And then the Capital."

"Preparing your mind to be someone else."

"Exactly." I glanced sideways at the tall black wing. He walked with his eyes forward, his shoulders square, his spine straight. Like the woods bent to his will. "Do you ever pretend to be someone else, General?"

He paused, coming to a halt at my question. Then, he continued walking along beside me. "No one has ever asked me that before."

"You were the Pureblood Heir. Tethered to a Cza who knew you were his greatest rival. It could not have been easy."

"It was not easy. But it was what it was."

"Did you pretend? Pretend to love him when you served?"

"Love is not needed in Crylia. It was not required."

"Did you pretend to respect him, then?"

"That's called duty, Em. To serve someone even though you don't want to."

Oh, I knew duty very well. Perhaps just as much as Nkita. "Did you really think Crylia were superior to humans, Nkita? Before you met me?"

"I still think it, Em. In some matters. But no longer in all of them."

"Cryl be damned, you don't have to be so honest."

"Some of us prefer it."

I would have seethed at the slight if I hadn't known Nkita was keeping a plethora of secrets from me. "In what ways do you now see Tru as superior? I'm curious."

"If ever you weren't curious, I'd call a physician."

"Don't dodge my question. You are the one who goaded me into a conversation when I was content with silence."

He sighed. "Tru are lighter footed. They have worse eyesight but steadier hands for archery—unless they are too emotional, of course—but their intuition is brilliant. They...listen. It is perhaps their greatest strength. Listen to the land, to the water, to one another. Also, the Tru work well with each other. There is not so much rivalry and politics. Everyone works. Everyone has a place, and no place is more valuable. Not even royalty."

I smiled. "You have been paying attention."

"I have." He made sure not to look at me as he continued. "But, they will still lose. The Crylia will destroy the Tru."

I shivered, tucking my hands under my arms to warm them. "Why, Nkita? Why fight the Tru?" I made sure not to give away too much of what I knew. "I don't understand."

"Secrets and stories, Em. Secrets and stories."

"So...you won't tell me."

"You choose to tell me yours, of your own will, and perhaps I'll share a few of mine."

I glared at the side of his perfect head. "Are you aware of how severely I dislike you at times?"

"Mm. Keeps me going on rather cold nights, actually."

By the time we made it to Yogdn, I had a new set of blisters and thighs so sore I could barely bend my legs. Nkita, however, seemed fine, his jaw still chiseled and his fists clenched at his sides for no reason. We walked into a small house on the outskirts of the town, and Nkita set his sword on the table.

"You are being occupied," he said loudly.

I stared, blinking. I hadn't realized I'd never seen a First General walk into a Cryl home before, except for Dagon's when no one was there.

A young white wing female stepped out of a room, looked at Nkita, and then disappeared once more. *Perhaps she's gone to make the house less dreary.* The windows were boarded, the walls a bleak and dark brown, the furniture bare and plain. Everything was spotless. Not usual for a woodland house, I'd come to find. I was expecting muddy footprints and puddles of old ale everywhere.

The female reappeared and bowed to Nkita. Then she stood, her hands folded before her, and waited.

I noticed the light glint off her Grounded ring and realized, white wing or not, she was not going to speak to Nkita unless he asked her to.

"Who owns this house?" Nkita asked.

The female's wide eyes darted between us. "My uncle."

"Where is he?"

"Out. He will return soon."

"We will wait," Nkita replied.

The young female, her white, gossamer hair straight and thick around her shoulders, trembled. If she had wings, her feathers would have ruffled. "Shall"—she had to clear her throat. "Shall I make myself available for the Grand Teth?"

I wanted to cry out that her question was ridiculous, but I held my tongue. I too was Grounded. She would think it unbelievable that I'd speak out against Nkita. Besides, I didn't have to worry, and neither did she. *He would never—*

"Yes. Go. Make preparations for me."

I stared at him, attempting to keep my mouth from flopping open in shock.

The female white wing blushed and bowed, nearly running into the door post as she turned and exited the main room of the home.

"Worry not, Em," Nkita said, removing his gloves and handing them to me. "You can wait here. We won't be long."

26

The Day The  Spy Lost Her Mind

Oh, this won't be a problem. I pulled my matted, tangled hair back and knotted it at the base of my neck. *I'll just kill him.*

I took one big step forward, but a hushed voice from behind stopped me in my tracks.

"Are you reporting for work?"

I almost said, 'No, I am murdering my mate, pardon me,' but swallowed those words and found appropriate ones. "We are visiting."

"We?" The silver wing's right eye twitched as he looked me over.

I'd never seen a silver wing before. They were nearly as rare as gold wings, and to find one on the outskirts of little, smelly Yogdn was unfathomable. But there he was. A pointed nose, narrow eyes that turned up at the far corners, and thin lips held in a serious, straight line on his slim face. He was tall but rather thin, his wings tucked so I could not see them. He kept his hair in long silvery braids, and his skin was a rich, iridescent copper.

"My...my mate. He's here." *No, he's not. He's in there with some female Cryl taking his final breaths.* "He's—"

The silver wing's grip on his stack of books tightened. "With...my offspring, then?" He cleared his throat. "I knew the Grand Teth was coming. I should have...I should have had her more prepared for it."

"You're alright with this?" I asked far too boldly. "With him taking your offspring? Just like that?"

"She's of age—"

"Oh yes, alright, perfect, *wonderful*. That's all that's required. A female to be of age and then any Cryl with a title can come plow her over. You know what? Why don't you stand there with your books like an absolute bloodplucking knobsucker, and I will go save her from all of your entitled stupidity."

I huffed off, stomping through the house to make sure everyone could hear me coming. I'd definitely not yielded or succumbed or whatever it was Rhaza had warned I do when it came to my mate.

I kicked open the doors to several rooms in my search, finding emptiness in each. "Nkita Opas! You'd better prepare yourself to come face to face with your most grave mistake! I am your nightmare, black wing!"

"Are you now?"

I swiveled in the short corridor, my fists shaking at my sides as I squared my stance, and narrowed my eyes as I faced him. "You."

Nkita smirked. "Hello, Nightmare."

"What are you—why are you—?"

He shrugged. "I saw an opportunity, is all."

"To pleasure yourself atop some young white wing?!"

"To see what you would do."

My cheeks were so hot, they hurt. "Kill you."

"Jealous, then?"

"Nkita, you've lost your mind."

He crossed the corridor, gripped my hair with one hand, sank his fingers into the flesh of my rear with the other, and walked me backward into one of the empty rooms. "Admit it."

My breath came in ragged bursts as I struggled against him. I had no choice but to look up into his face as he held me against him. "I've never been more angry with anyone in my life. I will admit nothing to you. Nothing."

"Admit that you were jealous because you love me. That you're angry because you feel what I do."

"If you felt what I feel right now, General, you would run and hide."

"I'm not afraid of your weak little arms, Nightmare. What are you going to do? Caress me to death?"

"I'm going to bleed you out in your sleep."

"I'll be waiting, then." He released me, and I stumbled backward. "Come on. Let's greet our hosts. I have to explain to them why my Teth-wed mate has a problem with her own customs."

He left me standing in that room, fuming, near to screaming. It was a cruel trick to play. And for what? To have me confess that I loved him the way he loved me? Was not my devotion enough? Was not my naked body beneath him whenever he desired enough? Was not my willingness to go along with his stupid lies and secret manipulations enough?

"Are you...alright?" the young white wing asked, standing before the ruined door to the room with wide eyes.

"No," I snapped.

"I...am sorry."

"It's not your fault, you pretty thing. It's mine." I crossed my arms with a scowl. "I've let my mate think he's king of Miror."

"Oh my," she gasped, unsure of what else to say.

"Don't worry. I'll put him in his place. Rebel King my whole entire arse." I looked to her, determination coursing through my stubborn Tru-ori veins. "I need to come up with a plan," I said, a devious flash in my eyes. Then I bowed, remembering I was supposed to be playing a part. "And you have a lovely home...?"

"Tahlya."

"Tahlya. Yes. I am Syiva." I smoothed my hair back, realizing I must have looked like chaos incarnate. "Would you mind terribly helping me to crush the heart of my black wing mate into a fine powder? For his own good, when the time comes?"

"Oh." She shrugged, her voice still timid. "If it would help the cause?"

"It most certainly would." I smiled. "Long live the Pureblood Heir."

27

The Day The Silver Wing Served

I shuddered as the smell of sour cabbage and spoiled eggs filled the house, curling around our bodies as we sat at the neat wooden table the next day.

Tahlya did her best to appear composed as she set glasses of ale before us but she gagged every few moments. "I...hope everything...is to your liking," she managed between breaths, her eyes watering. "We want you to feel rested before you depart for the Capital. Anything for the cause."

"Anything but *this*," Nkita mumbled with a frown.

I glared at him. "We're thankful for your hospitality, Tahlya. We know it's dangerous to host us this way." I left out the parts about the Hresh destroying the Queen's Home or the Crylia army annihilating most of the Tru territory or Rizel going full monster in order to apprehend Miasi and me...or Dagon playing hide-and-go-stab with Nkita every chance he got. "You are so kind."

"And...here we are," the silver wing interrupted, stumbling out of the kitchen area. "Now, you must forgive me. I am not the best cook by any means. I am especially poor at the parts that require flavor."

"That's the *whole part*," Nkita grumbled, scraping his fingers across the table in frustration.

I nudged his knee with mine. "Behave," I hissed. "You are supposed to be a Grand Teth with all your fancy manners. You should know better."

"Grand Teth only have fancy manners when we eat fancy food, Em," he hissed back. "I am offended."

"I've seen you wrangle snakes and roast them whole over fires, crunching their spines between your teeth," I whispered.

"Elevated fare compared to this."

I sighed, leaning back in my chair and smiling at the silver wing. "We appreciate the effort. Let's eat."

"Oh, we could never sit with the Pureblood Heir and his mate. We're not worthy of such company. I will attend to my work—work which I am much better suited for, thank Gua."

I held my amazement back and put a befuddled look on my face, more suited for a Crylia. "Did you just... thank...*Gua*? Is that not the Tru deity?"

"Ah yes," the silver wing said with a nod. "I have been studying the cultures of our enemies for some time. I am more trying the phrase out than anything else. Excuse my tactics."

"Tacticians are always peculiar," Nkita said, "but we are fortunate to have a silver wing such as yourself among the rebels."

I looked sideways at Nkita, knowing full well that he did not care for the rebel cause. *With all his talk of honesty and its virtues, he is such a marvelous liar.*

"If you have any needs, my offspring will tend to you. Tahlya, stay vigilant in case they call for you."

"I will," she said with a bow before disappearing into the kitchen. She poked her head back out to add, "I would start with the cabbage," she whispered, her eyes wide.

"Not the eggs?" I asked.

"No." Her eyes widened even further. "Not the eggs."

Nkita sighed once we were alone. "I did not miss this part. Having to put on airs around Cryl," he confessed. "At least with the Tru, I could say what I wanted."

"Because you didn't care what they thought of you."

"Because the Tru don't care about pretenses. It's refreshing."

I clenched my jaw and glared at him. "So glad you were refreshed."

"Em, you can't still be cross. You wouldn't even sleep near me last night."

"I might never sleep near you again."

"Or...you could just confess."

"You'll die an old old Cryl still wondering how I feel about you, First General."

"Then you'll die an old Tru too afraid to tell me the truth."

"You could have just asked."

"I did ask. More than once."

"You make no sense."

He banged his fist on the table, making the boiled eggs jiggle. "Here we go."

"You refuse to extract information from me about my life until I am ready to give it freely, yet you demand I make this confession of love to you on your terms, not mine. The dichotomy is maddening."

He bit his lip. "Is it truly so hard?"

"Perhaps I am truly so stubborn. Regardless of why I withhold, you shouldn't force me or deceive me into things, Nkita."

He crossed his bulky arms. "You're right."

"I am right and I am tired, and you are mean and handsome—wait, that's not what I meant to say—"

He looked me over. "I'm wrong for forcing you to confess?"

"Yes."

"And what if I told you I do not care?"

I swallowed. I didn't expect him to say that. "Why are you just...saying all these crass things, Nkita? You used to—"

"Choose my words more carefully. But I am wrong and I am tired, and you are mean and beautiful. And I'm not in the business of impressing you, woman. I want what I want." He stood up, his chair scraping against the hardwood. I knew if he had both his wings, he'd disappear into the gray clouds and come back whenever he felt like it. "I'm going to hunt some real food. Enjoy the shite you keep forcing yourself to swallow, Em."

I threw my hands into the air. "How am I being made into the villain in this exchange?! How?!" I growled, standing up from the table. "Ruthless, Em. Do not simply take this. Do something." *Make him pay. Make him learn.* And suddenly, I knew exactly what would teach Nkita Opas a lesson.

28

The Day The  Tree Opened

"Here are the plans," I told Tahlya. "You are going to make it seem as though I've left."

"But...you've only just arrived. We are supposed to prepare for your treacherous journey to the Capital." She blinked at me. "I still cannot believe the future Queen is a Grounded Crylia like me. I...don't know how to understand—"

"Yes, yes, that's very monumental." I put my hand on her shoulder. "But what's most important right now is payback, my white wing friend."

"My father told me I am to finish stitching your gowns—"

"You are very dutiful. However, Nkita Opas thought it wise to play a terrible trick on me, and I need to pay him back, or he will think I love him and I can't have that."

"You...can't love your mate?"

"No, I love him very much. It's quite ridiculous how much, but I can't let him know that. We must make it seem as if I don't so he doesn't grow too confident in my affection for him."

Tahlya wrinkled her nose. "I am afraid I don't understand how this helps the cause."

I sighed. "Just tell him you don't know where I've gone."

"If you don't tell me where you're going, Queen Syiva, I truly won't know."

"Oh. That's right. Well then." I cleared my throat. "I'm running away and I have no plans to return."

The female shivered. "This is all so troubling."

"It is. I hope he's devastated because I am rather tired and would like to not run away right now. But he's really left me no choice."

I gathered myself, stuffed my sore feet back into my boots, and slipped out the rear door, hustling toward the tree line. I made it a few minutes into the woods before I heard mumbling and slinked behind one of the snow-laden trees.

Who is out here in the cold? And what are they doing?

I peeked, keeping my body hidden. It was the silver wing, having a rather lengthy conversation with...the sturdy trunk of a tree.

What in the name of madness?

"Is that a spy I sense lurking behind me?"

I gasped, biting my lip. Then, I steadied myself. "Am I truly losing my touch?" I asked him. "I thought I'd be more difficult to detect."

"I am accustomed to solitude," he explained. "When there are eyes on me, I can sense the difference. Why don't you come out, future Queen. I will show you what I am up to."

I stepped out from my hiding, distracted from my plight for revenge for a time by the curiosities the silver wing presented. "I know very little of silver wings. I would love to learn more." The information could prove useful. Especially if it was about Crylia relations to our goddess or about the Vessels and Tonguekeepers, about the Zenith.

"We gold wings and silver wings are of the rarest sort. I am not surprised you know so little. But...we are rumored to get along well." He waited until I stood beside him. "I will show you, Syiva, in case ever you need an escape. Silver wings are few, but we are resourceful." He mumbled in Old Cryl. "It's not an incantation. We are no Tonguekeepers. It is just to remember the code for the entrance."

"Entrance?"

"*Voit-aya drevisnya a-ya veit e santas e vorosa*. Into the wood by the third time around, on the second day, of the fourth year." He sprouted talons from his fingertips and stuck them into the bark of the tree, where the tiniest holes already existed. The third hole, then the second, then the fourth, ignoring the many other holes that remained.

To my amazement, the tree groaned and a tiny latch revealed itself, carved from the heart of the trunk beneath its bark. The silver wing pulled it, and something creaked beneath our feet.

"Step aside," he said calmly. He knelt and dusted snow and leaves off a hatch door on the ground. "It is unlocked now."

"You have a hideaway!" I cried. "How clever."

"If you wish, I will show you what lies inside."

"Gladly. Thank you." *Nkita will never find me under there.* I followed the silver wing inside and realized I did not even know his name. "Pray tell, what should I call you?"

"Grigor is my name."

"Thank you. Grigor it is."

Midway down the rough ladder, the silver wing paused. When he landed at the bottom, he spoke with a bit more strain, his brow furrowed. "I forgot to mention...I do keep one of my offspring down here."

I froze in place, my hands on the ladder. "You... you what?"

"She's female. Older than Tahlya. But her presence here can be frightening to those who do not understand the context. I thought I should mention it before you descend, lest you decide you'd rather not enter my study."

I swallowed and climbed the rest of the way down. "No, no. It's quite alright. I...should like to see." *If that daughter needs my help, I will need to know where she is.* I hadn't quite decided if this Grigor was to be trusted, but the churning of my stomach indicated I ought to keep my guard up. "Please, lead the way."

The hollowed space beneath the tree was lit by slow burning candles. The walls hosted shelves carved out of stone and were crowded with books, tomes, and scrolls. A table of hand-carved wood was covered in quills and blank pages.

"You do your work in hiding?"

"I do. I...must. We keep information the Cza wishes we wouldn't. If he knew, all these manuscripts would be destroyed, and it is my purpose to hold all this knowledge. To collect it. To preserve it and transfer it."

"Your white wing daughters, they have different purposes?" I traced my fingers along the carefully etched covers of the leather bound books, my eyes collecting and retaining information of my own. He entered the study often. Kept it clean. No dust gathered on the shelves. The pages weren't cracked or yellowed. These were his treasures. This was, in a Cryl sort of way, his place of worship.

"Tahlya would make for a fine Capital white wing... if she had the stamina and cunning for politics. And then, of course, there is the nature of being a Grounded. But she is a gentle thing. I am glad the First General did not take advantage of the custom of occupancy. That would have burdened me greatly."

Oh, Nkita wouldn't have dared. But it was good to know at least the silver wing would have been upset, even if he was prepared to let it happen. "And...Tahlya's sister?" I shivered as I imagined this calm, demure silver wing who loved knowledge squeezing rations through rusted bars to feed his own offspring. "Her purpose? You say you keep her locked here?"

"She...her mother left her on my doorstep as an egg. It has been difficult raising her, I must confess."

And so you jailed her underground? "I see."

"Perhaps...perhaps you might know what I can do. Gold wings are especially intuitive, where we silver wings are sometimes *too* logical."

We made our way to the back of the hollowed study and found a cell of sorts, the metal bars wrapped with cloths of lovely colors and designs. Within sat a female, just a bit older than Tahlya by her looks. Her freckled skin shone even in the low light, and her red eyes matched long scarlet tresses.

"A...a red wing?"

"This is Ikyi." He took a shallow breath, as if bracing himself. "Ikyi, perhaps you can greet our new guest as we've rehearsed?"

The red wing narrowed her eyes at me. "By driving my talons into her pathetic, pulsing little heart and squeezing until her warm blood gushes between my fingers?"

"Ah," I said with a nod. "I see your problem, Grigor."

She locked her shimmering ruby eyes on me and smiled, her tongue lagging out for a moment before she spoke. "And I see mine."

29

The Day The Silver Wing Taught

"Ikyi, please. We must refine our tongues. We are in the presence of Crylia greatness."

The red wing's eyes shone. "I love greatness. Nice crunch to it." She licked her lips, curling her fingers around the bars. "Don't you want to take me home, Greatness? I'd be a good little playmate for you...."

I knelt before the bars, careful not to get too close. "Ikyi Red Wing...I have a question for you."

She pressed her pretty face against the bars as if she was trying to squeeze through. "For me?"

"Yes." I took a deep breath. "Do you want to be set free?"

"She cannot—" Grigor began.

I held up my hand to silence him. "I am talking to Ikyi."

She chuckled. "I hate it in this awful cage. You want to let me out?"

"I will discuss it with your father."

She tossed a wicked glare towards Grigor. "That Cryl is *not* my father."

"He...*isn't?*"

"I have no father. I have no mother. I belong to no one. But I could belong to you if you wanted me. Do you want me?"

I stood, straightening up, and left the area where the young monster was being held, leaning my palms against Grigor's table.

"You must understand, I am not intending cruelty by leaving Ikyi—"

"I am not interested in your excuses. Only in your reasoning."

He frowned, surprised. "Oh?"

"Are all red wings so absolutely unhinged?"

"Most are, yes. But they can be...tamed. In a sense. In part."

"And you have her here to tame her? That's your goal?"

He shook his head. "It would take a terrible master to do that. Someone who understands punishment, command. One who can break them. And then...to an extent...they become more useful. But—"

"You don't wish that fate for your offspring?"

"If the Cza—"

"Feigning Cza."

"Ah, that is a lovely way to say it. The Feigning Cza...he would use Ikyi. Ruin her. Break her spirit and her body.

I cannot let her free, not only because she is a danger to others, but because this world is a danger to her."

"And if, let's say, a General and a red wing were...friends? How could something like that come about?"

Grigor blinked. "Friends?"

"Friends."

"I...don't think that's possible. Red wings do not make alliances. They do not have friends. They don't know duty or loyalty. They can only be conditioned to obey, but it is not because they want to."

I nodded. *So whatever Nkita and Dagon have between them...it's not usual. Well, clearly it's not usual, as they are insane. But even more so, it is unprecedented.*

"Grigor Silver Wing? Might I inquire as to something else?"

"My mind is at your service, Queen Syiva."

"I was raised on the edge of Crylia, in a small town even beyond the Woodlands. I know very little about weaponry and armor, but it pleases the Pureblood Heir that I am educated in these ways."

Grigor nodded. It was unusual for a Crylia female to inquire into matters such as weaponry. "I see. The *Krov vanya crystin* is as unusual as he is wise. What questions do you have?"

"Your long swords? What are they called?"

"*Deliniv mech*. Blades that go on. They are usually wielded by those with strong arms and wide stances."

"And the shorter ones? I see rebel females with those."

Grigor fetched a book and thumbed through the pages. "This will help you visualize." He stopped at a particular page and showed me the blade I'd asked about. "*Sredniy mech*. For shorter arms who can still wield a heavy sword."

I angled the book toward him and flipped until I found the section on daggers. Then I pointed and put on my most innocent, ignorant voice. "What about something like this? But more...gnarled. Twisted."

His eyes flicked up to me. "A...a twisted blade, you say?"

"Mhmm. I heard someone mumbling about it once when I passed through Led. They said a twisted blade would be worth killing for, but that no one would ever find anything like it ever again. What...could they have meant?"

Grigor hesitated, then hurried off to his shelves, returning with another bound tome. He located a new page and tapped it. "It is in Old Cryl," he explained.

"I am not so good with the ancient tongue. Forgive me."

"No, you wouldn't have learned so far away from the Capital. But"—he showed me the ornate drawing of the blade Umra had traded me for. The one that had brought on the death of Letti and her killer, leaving only one Vessel behind. The blade that sealed my fate as the next Tonguekeeper.

"What's it for?" I asked.

"It is a sacred blade. The most sacred. *Klinok mech*. Crylia mythos says that its power comes from the very foundation of Miror. That it was cut by the first maker of the blades, the one who cut and shaped the very mountains of this world. And that he made it for his first and only love...the first Tonguekeeper."

"Who...do you think she was? What was she like?"

"Some believe she was just a Cryl. Some that she was a Ven. Some that she was a Bahari. And some say she was a mere human."

I laughed. "A *human*? That would be ridiculously simple, wouldn't it?"

"There are powers that cannot exist unless they are in balance, Queen Syiva. Humans play their role, just as we all do."

"I suppose. Poor things. I always feel sorry for them."

"Perhaps one day, a human will feel sorry for you."

"What did you say?"

Grigor shook his head. "Queen Syiva, I must return to my work. But, I have given you the code to our silver wing studies. Many have been built in Crylia and house our knowledge. They can house you as well if ever you need, but please...tell no one."

"I am honored, Grigor. I will treasure the secret." I glanced over his shoulder, toward the cell where Ikyi was loudly snoring. "All your secrets."

"Anything," Grigor said, "for the cause. I am sure your mate must be looking for you by now."

Good. I hope he thinks I've left him. I hope he is enraged. That will teach him a lesson.

30

THE DAY THE  SPY CONFESSED

I exited the cellar of a study, and my skin prickled. *My black wing.*

"Pretending you do not notice me standing here?" His tone was sharp, his voice deep. I could tell how upset he was before I even looked at him. When I did look at him, I had to bite my lip to keep from gasping.

He was beautiful in the early afternoon light, gray and hazy as it was. Dark hair clean and falling to his shoulders, jaw sharp and freshly shaven, lilac eyes glittering and glaring.

"Thought you'd be scouring the forest looking for me by now."

"I knew you were close. Hiding. But close."

"I'll have to run away with a bit more effort next time."

"You know, there are ways to sever our bond, Em."

I swallowed, looking around to make sure Grigor had not followed. Then, I approached Nkita and put my hand on his arm. "First General"—I had to force my words out—"what are you saying? Is that what you want?"

"Is that what you want?"

"No!" I shook my head, panic shooting through my body as I contemplated what he was suggesting. "Why...if I wanted that, I could have done it already." I squeezed his arm. "Nkita, I thought we were...being...ourselves. I didn't know you were truly so upset with me—you want me gone?"

"Of course not!"

"Then why would you suggest it?"

"Because you're running from me. Again."

"I was being troublesome, Nkita. That's all. Goodness, you'd think I'd have run a little farther! Picked up the pace a bit!"

"So you want this. You choose this."

"Yes, I choose this. Alright? Are you happy now?"

"Not in the slightest."

"Nkita—" My words were cut short when he pulled his arm away from me.

"Enough of our games, Emyri. It's time to go."

"Go...to the Capital? Nkita, I have questions before we go."

"I'm sure you do. You always do."

"I don't want Drosya hurt."

"That's not a question."

"How can we make sure she's not killed in this process?"

"We can't. And I won't."

I exhaled, frustrated but trying to remain calm. "You're going to use the twisted blade to do it? Sneak into the castle and kill Drosya? Going to make me the Tongue-keeper so that I can convince the Zenith to choose you?"

"What do *you* know of the Zenith?"

"We can convince her, Nkita. To be on our side. She...she likes me. At least, I think she does. Just promise me that you'll try."

"I am quite tired of being forced into compassion because I chose a human as my mate."

"I am quite tired of having to beg for it! But I am begging. And you did choose me. Neither of us are walking away from this, Nkita Opas. Love does not work that way."

He stepped forward without warning so that I gasped again and gripped my throat with a strong hand. Without hesitation, I put my fingers on his neck and held. We were eye to eye. Chest to chest.

"You love me. You chose me. I'm your mate in truth?"

I swallowed against the pressure of his palm, his fingers. "And I always will. No matter how much of an arse you happen to be. You're stuck with me, One Wing."

"You feel me. When we're apart?"

"And it hurts. Like Gua's forsaken me and my insides are being bruised with a club."

"Good." I expected a kiss, but my mate only nodded. "We need to make haste."

Make...haste? I just confessed what he's been demanding I tell him, and that's all he is going to say? We need to make haste? "Nkita—"

But he was already moving, his long black cape, fresh and new, billowing behind him. His boots were freshly polished, his armor gleaming.

"The white wing female will bathe and dress you. Do not waste time."

I muttered complaints under my breath as I made it back to the house and let Tahlya strip me down and scrub me. I hated letting others bathe me but I was too distracted by the changes I was seeing in my mate to let myself fight off the Crylia customs.

Tahlya dressed me in a shimmering dress of gold that flowed off my limbs like a silken waterfall. The fabric strategically covered all my bruises and even the scars on my back. She knit fine gold necklaces through my fingers, draping them up my arms and around my neck, tucking them into the woven crown of my braids. Then, carefully, she slipped a slender golden ring into my bottom lip.

"Not silver?" I asked, surprised.

"Something special. To denote you are not like other Grounded."

"But...I am like other Grounded," I assured her.

She glanced up at me in awe. "You are nothing like us, Queen Syiva. You are something more."

And that something more was put in a carriage and jostled all the way to the heart of the Capital of Crylia, past the roads where I'd slipped and sneaked to deliver messages to the Tru, past the houses that contained the secrets of the Grand Teth and the nobles, where I'd scrubbed floors and intercepted messages. I bit my lip as I saw in the distance the house where I'd first met the General. He'd landed with heavy boots and seen through my ruse immediately. I hadn't known love would come next. Or what dangers there were for me. Or that a twisted blade would change my fate forever.

"Pick up the pace," Nkita called to the driver. "There is much to be done."

31

The Day The  Carriage Arrived

The carriage stopped, and my heart stopped with it. The castle loomed above us, stone-gray spires crafted out of granite staring down at me, condemning me. Threatening me. *You are not welcomed,* the castle said. *You weak little human. You should run.*

"Em...we must get out of the carriage," Nkita said, his voice unusually soft.

"I am," I told him.

"What you are doing is ripping holes into my arm."

"Oh," I said. I'd been digging my fingernails into his wrist, taking full advantage of the gap in his armor. "I...."

"You're afraid?"

"Me? No. I am beyond terrified. The last time I stepped out of a carriage like this—the last time...Nkita, I don't think I understand. We have been running from the Cza for so long. Now we are simply...walking into the castle?

He will kill you for betraying him. He will use me against you...again."

"Emyri Izela?"

"Nkita Opas?"

"Do you remember what we did before we got out of that carriage the last time we arrived at this castle?"

Without warning, heat shot through my legs, traveling up my thighs to my center. "I...do...but—"

Nkita moved, his armor clanging as he unfastened his breast plate and set it aside. He slipped his hands across my back, his fingers pressing against my spine as he pulled me to him. He kissed me slowly, carefully, his tongue confident. Then, he looked into my eyes.

"Can you trust me, Em?"

I touched my palms to the sides of his face, straddling him in the carriage and trying to remember to breathe. "I'll try, General. That is the best I can give you."

He nodded. "I'll take it."

He slid his hands up my thighs, caressing my skin as they made their way beneath my dress. He let me unfasten the buttons of his trousers, then he gripped my rear and pulled me down onto him until I inhaled against the sensation.

"I'll take it, Em," he said again.

And I let my tense body relax, let my muscles find his rhythm and my heart slow to mimic his. Whatever separation there was between the two of us slowly melted, like the mounds of snow along the border between our territories—Crylia and Tru, perhaps, were not so different after all.

"Stay with me," Nkita said, moving deeper than I thought possible. "Em, stay."

I wanted to. I wanted to let go of everything I'd held back. To fall to pieces in his arms. To sob against his neck and tell him how scared I'd been every single day and how much I missed the ones I loved. I wanted to confess the toll that lying took on me and how it made my very soul bleed. How I couldn't stop. How the lies were simply part of me now, my way of life.

But I couldn't find the words and I couldn't find the way to let go of it all, try as I might. I was still Emyri, and she was still...broken.

Emotion wrecked my body, heat and ecstasy flooding through me in a raging torment as we finished. Tears slipped down my cheeks. "I'm...sorry," I whispered. Barely a whisper. "I love you and I'm sorry it's not good enough—"

He wiped my tears away, kissed my cheeks. "I love you, Em, and I'll *take it*."

The carriage door went flying off its hinges, and Nkita pulled a dagger, aiming it at whomever meant us harm, pushing me so I fell to the floor of the carriage behind him.

"How long was I to stand there waiting for you, hm?"

The black wing scowled, his dark feathers spread wide behind him, his hand on the hilt of the sword at his waist.

"Rizel."

"Opas."

"Back away from our carriage."

Rizel smirked. "Have you come to grovel before the Cza? I'd laugh at how piteous you look, but that would make me a hypocrite. I did not last long without him either, Nkita. It can't be helped."

Grovel? Are we here to...grovel?

"I am here for an audience with the Cza," Nkita said. "The reasons are not for you to concern yourself with, Rizel. Let him know I've arrived."

Rizel glanced past Nkita, his dark eyes landing on me. "You didn't even bring him the Tru Queen? Pathetic?"

"You didn't bring her in either," I snapped. "How did you manage to regain the Cza's favor?"

Rizel's eye twitched, the veins in his forehead throbbing as he beheld me. "As if you're owed answers. The only reason I didn't tear you to shreds, puny Grounded, is because I want to see the look on General Nkita's face when the Cza offers you to me in front of him."

I waited, braced myself, ready for Nkita to unleash his wrath on the wicked black wing.

But...he did not.

Instead, with his jaw clenched, he growled, "Tell the Cza...I am here."

He stepped out of the carriage after Rizel left and turned back toward me, outstretching his hand. "Come with me."

I more than hesitated, my hands balled into fists held against my chest as I sat scrunched on the floor of the carriage. I trembled, my words deserting me. *What is happening? What could possibly be happening?*

"Emyri Izela," Nkita said again. "*Come.*"

What are your options, Em? You can't run. He'd catch you. Would he chase you down though? Yes. He's done it before. I swallowed, trying to stop from shaking like a squirrel in a cage. *What reason do you have to distrust him, Em? He's always been valiant on your behalf. Always. And you feel what he feels...when you're apart. He wants you. He...he loves you.*

I unfurled my fingers, inched toward the edge of the carriage, and took the General's hand.

32

The Day The Spy Overheard

There was no Rhaza to greet us as we entered the castle of the Great Cza of Crylia. Not this time. The halls were filled with servants and nobles, each doing the work they were assigned, each bent toward the will of the king in some fashion.

The cold was setting in, which meant the ceilings of the castle were drawn into place. No longer could winged monsters flit in and out through the heavens. Instead, they used narrow windows to come and go, moving with speed and precision.

The white wing nobles took graceful steps as they moved from political conversation to political conversation, their females gliding about and trying their best to draw attention to themselves. No black wings mulled in the halls. If they were present, no doubt they were plotting strategies or training for battle somewhere we could not see. I suspected most of them were out waging war, though, hunting the few surviving Tru that were left after their last raid. I hoped my sister and friends were among the survivors. But there was little time for hope. That, I would leave up to Gua.

There were whispers as we passed by. Eyes turning toward us. I fell behind a ways, as I should have, and Nkita took the lead, his steps meaningful and his being resonating with power.

I need answers. My breath quickened the closer we got to the Cza's throne room. *I need answers. I can't do this without knowing why I'm here. Without knowing what my mate has planned.*

A servant met us, bowing briefly and keeping her eyes downcast. "This way," she whispered. "The Cza will meet with you soon."

She led us into a room with ornate dressings of ivory and blue, gold trimmings glittering on the furniture, walls, and ceiling. The servant poured Nkita a drink—none for me, of course—and bowed before she left.

I put a hand to my stomach to steady my nerves. "Nkita, please—"

"This part is almost over, Em."

"What...what part? *What part?!*"

"Keep your *voice down*—"

"I—"

The door opened, and the servant bowed her apology. "The Great Cza will see you." Then she gestured to Nkita. "Alone, First General."

Out of instinct, I grabbed Nkita's hand. *Don't go. Don't.*

He turned back to me and kissed me, his lips pressed against mine like it was his last taste, like I was his last breath. He tilted my head up so I could see only him. "You stay right here, Nightmare. *Right. Here.* And wait for me."

Before I could say another word, my General left me all alone, the door to the small room closing behind him.

I paced, hoping the motion would keep me from getting sick all over the Cza's floor, but it did little to quell my fears. The last time Nkita had left me in a tiny room in this castle, I was left trembling for weeks with no one but Mlika White Wing to help me, waiting for Nkita to drag his bleeding body back to me.

When at last I could take the waiting no longer, I looked for a way out. Rooms meant for prisoners would be secure, but these, with fine furnishings? They were meant for nobles. And if there was a siege, nobles would need a way to escape.

I traced my fingers along the wall, along whatever seems I could find. Until finally...*nothing*.

Frustrated, and without thinking, I made my way to the door as if I could simply follow my mate to his meeting with the Cza. To my complete shock, the door opened. I hadn't been locked in. I was simply expected to stay.

And so I did the exact opposite.

I waited until no one passed through the corridor and slipped out, closing the door behind me, careful to mark which one I'd come from. Sneaking, I rested my palm on doors to find if any were occupied. The low rumblings of voices meant Cryl were doing business in each of them.

I would have kept going this way until I found a place to hide, until I found a way out of the castle, if not for the voices I recognized on the other side of the last door. Muffled voices, yes. But I recognized Nkita's baritone anywhere.

With no one around, I dropped to the floor, my belly tight against the freezing stone. And I pressed my ear against the slit beneath the door. Listening. Doing what I did best. Spying.

"It is good to have you home," someone said. A male's voice, but higher. Smooth as ice.

"I am honored to be welcomed back," Nkita replied. "You are indeed gracious, Great Cza."

I had to bite my lip to bleeding to keep myself from gasping.

"And what of the Vessel," the Cza asked. "Have you persuaded her?"

"I have gained her trust. Just as you asked me to."

"The Zenith is not far off. All we need is for this rotting Tonguekeeper to pass her gift to your...mate."

"The Vessel is the only one who remains, my Cza. The Tonguekeeper will have no choice. And if she resists, she can be coerced."

"We must do this tactfully, Opas. If it appears your mate is under duress, the Zenith will revolt against us. It must be flawless. She must choose me willingly."

"And she will. I have won her affection. Believe me. Humans are simple. And once they trust, they do so fully."

"I will repay you for your service one of these days, First General. When I am made the head of the Zenith and the time of the Tonguekeepers comes to an end."

"That, my Great Cza, will be reward enough. It is all I want. It is all I have ever wanted."

With tears burning my cheeks, I pulled myself to my feet and took haggard, hastened steps back to the room where my black wing had left me. For when he opened that door and looked into my eyes, I needed it to look like I wanted nothing more than to die in his arms, as if nothing had changed. Like I was simple. Like I was stupid. Like I was his.

Like it was all I'd ever wanted.

More
By Teshelle Combs

Scan to read the
The First Collection
And other books.

Review
This Book

Scan to leave a review for
REEDS FOR WIND

FROM THE MIND OF TESHELLE COMBS

The First
Collection

The First Dryad 1 & 2

A forbidden love, slow-burn, magically-enchanted romance

The First Stone

An enemies to lovers, arranged marriage, romantic adventure

The First Nymph

A haunting enemies to lovers, star-crossed, fantasy romance

The First Flame

A forbidden love, romantic action, royal drama

The First Breath

A fast burn, forbidden love, mystical, heartbreaking romance

The First Muse
A sweeping, age gap, classical romance

The First Dragon
A chaos-fueled, fated mates romance

The First Spark
A tantalizing tale of romantic obsession

The First Shadow
A twisted story of love and betrayal

The First Collection Reading Paths

The First Collection is a series of standalone novels woven together to create a cohesive fantasy romance experience. Choose your own path to piece together the puzzle, or select one of these 10 paths to curate a journey for your personality!

The Romantic

You are bound to love. Read it all in the most romantic flow, ending with a happily ever after.

1. The First Dryad 1
2. The First Spark
3. The First Muse
4. The First Nymph
5. The First Flame
6. The First Shadow
7. The First Breath
8. The First Dragon
9. The First Stone
10. The First Dryad 2

The Warrior

You are fearless. Attack the most soul-shattering stories first.

1. The First Breath
2. The First Nymph
3. The First Muse
4. The First Shadow
5. The First Dryad 1
6. The First Dryad 2
7. The First Spark
8. The First Flame
9. The First Dragon
10. The First Stone

The Adventurer

You crave a good epic tale. Read it all as one adventurous thrill.

1. The First Muse
2. The First Stone
3. The First Nymph
4. The First Spark
5. The First Flame
6. The First Breath
7. The First Dryad 1
8. The First Dryad 2
9. The First Dragon
10. The First Shadow

The Purist

You don't mess with perfection. Read in the exact order the books were written.

1. The First Dryad 1
2. The First Stone
3. The First Nymph
4. The First Flame
5. The First Dryad 2
6. The First Breath
7. The First Muse
8. The First Dragon
9. The First Spark
10. The First Shadow

The Elementalist

You are one with nature. Read with each element grouped together.

1. The First Flame
2. The First Dragon
3. The First Dryad 1
4. The First Dryad 2
5. The First Breath
6. The First Muse
7. The First Shadow
8. The First Spark
9. The First Stone
10. The First Nymph

The Historian

You are a defender of order. Read along with the true timeline of the overall story.

1. The First Breath
2. The First Stone
3. The First Flame
4. The First Dragon
5. The First Dryad 1
6. The First Dryad 2
7. The First Nymph
8. The First Muse
9. The First Shadow
10. The First Spark

The Scholar

You crave information. Read in the order that fills in the most details first.

1. The First Shadow
2. The First Dragon
3. The First Dryad 1
4. The First Dryad 2
5. The First Nymph
6. The First Breath
7. The First Stone
8. The First Muse
9. The First Flame
10. The First Spark

The Chaos

You like to tempt fate and tease your brain. Read in the most unnatural order possible.

1. The First Dragon
2. The First Spark
3. The First Muse
4. The First Nymph
5. The First Stone
6. The First Shadow
7. The First Dryad 2
8. The First Flame
9. The First Breath
10. The First Dryad 1

The Heartcrusher

You aren't afraid to cry. Read from happiest to most devastating.

1. The First Stone
2. The First Dragon
3. The First Flame
4. The First Spark
5. The First Dryad 1
6. The First Dryad 2
7. The First Shadow
8. The First Muse
9. The First Nymph
10. The First Breath

The Maverick

You don't color inside the lines. Choose your own journey in any order you wish!

Books
eBook and Paperback

brightless

But none of us spent a lot of time thinking about how the Lost became the Lost. We were more concerned with how to keep them from killing us, from taking us...or from corrupting us.

Their steps were not only silent, but quick, almost hovering over the ground, as if there was nothing holding them back any longer. I'd need to do my best to listen for them, to evade them as I darted through the camp and toward the open land where I hoped Bit had wandered to. This terrain was still new to us since the Line had just moved. I'd have to be careful. A few breaths were needed as I attempted to recall where the tents had been placed. We always tried to set things up the same, but new families joined us and old ones fell behind. Things changed.

"Struggle," My mother whispered, barely audible. She squeezed my good arm. "Iluma...Iluma bring you light."

I paused, my heart racing for some reason I did not understand. Maybe because I'd never heard my mother use that phrase. *It's something they must say up the Line.* It's something my mother was careful to have left behind her all these years. *So...why? Why say it now?*

Was she truly so afraid I'd be caught by the Lost and corrupted? That I'd Lose My Way too?

"I'll be fine," I told her.

She slipped something into my hand. A novaseed. I could feel its round edges as I shoved it into my pocket. Of all the ways to purchase light in the Back of the Line, novaseeds were some of the most effective. They held immense amounts of light when cracked open—enough to last the entire lifetime of the plant. Which meant I held in my sad little pocket the most expensive thing my family had ever owned. I shuddered to think what my mother must have traded to get it.

With the seed secured, I took off at a dead run, pushing past the tents and hoping to dart away from any Lost who were searching them. Maybe they wouldn't expect a young man to sprint by. As long as none of them touched me. As long as none of them held me. We didn't understand how they passed the Losing from person to person. We did know that if someone wandered too far from the camps for too long, they'd Lose Their Way without being corrupted. It just....happened.

Both ways of Losing were terrifying. But I was in danger from the first.

Books
eBook and Paperback

SEVER & SPLIT

His lips grazed my forehead, and everything else was quiet and still. If I lived to be one thousand years old, I would never feel as entirely wanted as I did in that moment.

"Era...when I said you shouldn't touch me.... Before. In the lodge. It wasn't because...I would never...." His words failed him. "I love it when you touch me, Era. I just want to make that perfectly clear."

I nodded my head.

Oteros tucked a loose strand of my hair behind my ear, and I made the mistake of looking up into his eyes. He made the mistake of letting his hand slip down to my neck and allowing his lips to meet mine. For a moment. Just a moment.

Everything...*sang*. It was as though the stars had turned to rain and the wind had turned to music. As if the rhythm of the land danced beneath my feet.

But there was something else. Something...hot and violent and unpredictable. Some part of me that I had always been told should never exist.

More. More now.

And I didn't have time to back away and blush sweetly, to tell Oteros we'd made a mistake. That we were friends and friends are careful with one another. Never reckless. No, I only had time to press myself against him and to thrust my fingers into his hair. To push my hips forward and to part his lips with my tongue.

"Era! Era, where are you?!"

It wasn't until I heard my sister calling from a distance that I pulled myself away from Oteros. I stumbled backward, my eyes locking with his.

"Era, wait—"

But I was gone. Stumbling down the path and away from whatever had overtaken me. I was meant to be solving problems. But it turned out, I was the biggest one of all.

Books
Kindle and Paperback

The Underglow

I confessed to myself that I had paid very little attention to the countless governesses who attempted to explain the general rules of romantic engagement for Femmes of my stature and upbringing. But despite my lack of knowledge of general rules, I had a general sense that I was breaking them, whatever they were. Generally speaking, of course.

Closer should have made me nervous. I was not nervous, however, and so closer I went until there was no separation between his hips and mine. This was a relief to me—one difficult to explain. For I did not think there could ever be such closeness between another living thing and myself. Truly, I did not think, though they claimed to desire it, that any other living thing wanted to be so close to me.

<<You withhold>>, Alexander meant to me, pulling my bottom lip between his before pressing his mouth fully to mine. I felt only the slightest prick of his fangs, for he had not lengthened them. With my head nearly swimming, I wondered if he would sink those fangs into me as he once did. But no. Instead, he intended. <<I will be patient>>.

I detested patience. It was a monster that society told its victims was required, but really, it only convinced us all to work longer hours while they fattened us up for the slaughter. What is the point of patience? Who does it serve but the impatient ones?

I wrapped my arms around his waist and held firmly, but he released my grip rather easily.

<<Patience>>. With a last touch of his thumb to my lip and a final probe of his considerate eyes, he stepped away. <<I will find who hurt you>>.

I truthfully thought he had forgotten about this, as it had left my mind entirely. The idea that he would seek some vengeance on my behalf made my hands go numb, for it led me to envision Alexander strung up in a dark dungeon, awaiting Sleep. Surely he would be captured. Surely he would be enslaved once more. Surely I would not be able to save him. Chivalry was not something I required from this pyre.

But he looked at me—some small distance between us—in such a way that I could not believe it was chivalry compelling him.

<<You do not wish me to find them>>, he meant. The feeling of his meaning came slow and hot, like waves against a stone on too warm of a day. Or like standing too close to a flame. This is what it felt like for Alexander to be cross with me.

I wondered if I should be worried that I enjoyed the feeling.

And then I felt a shift in him, or rather, felt it come from him. <<I will go>>.

Books
Kindle and Paperback

Slit Throat Saga Series

"My people," he said, yelling over the toning, "let's celebrate. For today, the one who breaks the laws of nature, the one who moves the unmovable, the one who tests the very hands of God, will be set back on the right path. The Fight is not in vain."

He turned with a flourish to watch with us all as a translucent synthetix blade, held tight in the Moral's fist, sliced across the throat of the girl. A gurgle, then her blonde head flopped forward. Her blood gushed brilliant red. One would think it meant that the Fight was mistaken, that she was just like everyone else—a normal human with no unearthly capabilities, no deadly tendencies. Her blood seemed pure and red, filled with iron just like it should be. But after a few seconds, as her strength faded, the red diluted and her blood ran clear as a mountain river.

She was Meta. Just like they thought and I'm sure as they determined when she was confined in the House of Certainty for questioning. No true metal in her veins. No metal in her whole body. Not even metal in her mind. Instead she could pull it to her. She was a magnet. An abomination. And if left uncaught and unkilled, her kind would destroy the world.

The people—my people—cheered along with the Best Of Us as the Meta's watery blood poured over her small breasts, down her loose linen shirt, over the wooden platform, and through the street. It always amazed me how long Meta could bleed, how much life they held in their bodies. We all waited until the flow pooled beneath our feet, Ender Stream blessing us with one final reminder: *If you are us, you live, and if you are them, you die.*

"Well, Nex," Onur said with a little sigh as the crowd began to disperse, shoes squelching in the remains of the Meta girl, "what must be done is done." He brushed my thick, silver curls behind my ear so he could kiss my temple again, his favorite habit. His pale skin seemed to shine against my dusty red complexion. He looked tired, but he smiled. "We should get something to eat, yes?"

I smiled back at him, turning and tiptoeing so I could reach his lips with my own. His were soft and yielding, warm and inviting. Mine were not quite as full, not quite as tender. I met his eyes, ensuring that my gaze said exactly what I needed it to. *All Fight, no fear.* "Yes, let's eat. We can say cheers to the next one to be found."

I stepped through the Stream, one hand tight in my love's. The other hand I kept stuffed in the pocket of my cotton dress, clenched, but not so firmly that my fingernails might draw blood from my palm. That would not do. For the Stream soaking through my shoes was no less damned than the blood coursing through my veins.

Careful, Nex.
Careful.

Books
Kindle and Paperback

Tuck Me In

I stepped toward him. "Marrow, you walked from There to Here? That must have taken hours. You could have been hurt. You could have been killed."

He nodded. "I did not know that when I set out, but I am aware of the dangers now. There were many."

"So you're not alright. Oh Dios." I rubbed my chest. My heart was definitely not stopped anymore. It raced, banging against its cage. "I might actually be sick."

"Bel...."

I smacked my hands together. "Marrow, what were you thinking?" He didn't answer. But I found the sadness growing in his dark eyes.

"I'm sorry I'm yelling," I said. And I was so sorry. He didn't know why I was so upset, why the thought of him coming all this way was nightmare-inducing rather than a wonderful surprise.

That's when, without being able to stop myself, I reached out and touched his elbow.

Now, I knew—I knew—I was not supposed to touch my subject. It was on every Grade test I had ever taken. We can't study something if we manipulate it. If we handle it. If we hold it.

But my hand on his elbow led to him leaning into me. He wrapped both arms around me and put his cheek to my hair. And he lingered. In his still, slow way.

I clutched the back of his shirt and pressed my face to his chest and fought the tears that came to my eyes.

"You're okay," he said calmly, with that voice that sounded like magic being born. Like a fantasy opening its eyes.

That was the first time I realized how much everything hurt, all the time, from every direction, and how much I wished it would all stop.

Everything, that is, except for a Glimpse named Marrow.

Books
Kindle and Paperback

Core Series

Ava is the kind of girl who knows what's real and what isn't. Nothing in life is fair. Nothing is given freely. Nothing is painless. Every foster kid can attest to those truths, and Ava lives them every day. But when she meets a family of dragon shifters and is chosen to join them as a rider, her very notion of reality is shaken. She doesn't believe she can let her guard down. She doesn't think she can let them in—especially not the reckless, kind-eyed Cale. To say yes to him means he would be hers—her dragon and her companion—for life. But what if Ava has no life left to give?

The System Series

1 + 1 = Dead. That's the only math that adds up when you're in the System. Everywhere Nick turns, he's surrounded by the inevitability of his own demise at the hands of the people who stole his life from him. That is, until those hands deliver the bleeding, feisty, eye-rolling Nessa Parker. Tasked with keeping his new partner alive, Nick must face all the ways he's died and all the things he's forgotten.

Nessa might as well give up. The moment she gets into that car, the moment she lays her hazel eyes on her new partner, her end begins. It doesn't matter that Nick Masters can slip through time by computing mathematical algorithms in his mind. It doesn't matter how dark and handsome and irresistibly cold he is. Nessa has to defeat her own shadows. Together and alone, Nick and Nessa make sense of their senseless fates and fight for the courage to change it all. Even if it means the System wins and they end up...

well...dead.

Poetry
Thoughts Like Words

Let There Be Nine Series
- *Let There Be Nine Vol 1*: **Enneagram Poetry**
- *Let There Be Nine Vol 2*: **Enneagram Poetry**

For Series: Words laced together on behalf of an idea, a place, a world.
- **For Her**
- **For Him**
- **For Them**
- **For Us**

Love Bad Series: Poems About Love. Not Love Poems.
- **Love Bad**
- **Love Bad More**
- **Love Bad Best**

Standalone Poetry Books:

Breath Like Glass

Poems for love that never lasts.

Girl Poet

A collection of poems on the passion, privilege, and pain of being (or not quite being) a girl.

FRAMELESS

A collection of poems for the colors that make life vibrant, from their perspective, so we may share in what they might think and feel.

This One Has Pockets

Narrative poetry about a girl who is near giving up and the boy who tries to save her.

ON THE NATURE OF HINGES

A series of poetic questions from the perspective of someone who has been left behind more than once.

Gray Child

A unique expression of being more than one race, written by a Caribbean American woman, for anyone who cares to read.

Contact Teshelle Combs

Instagram | @TeshelleCombs

Facebook | TC's Fantasy and Dystopian Readers

Leave A Review

A good review is how you breathe life into my story. Please leave REEDS FOR WIND an Amazon review and tell a friend how much you love Em and Nkita.

Made in the USA
Middletown, DE
29 July 2025

10906090R00118